The thought that he could have lost her today—had come so close to losing her— had him crushing her to him.

He wrapped one arm around her hips and threaded his other hand through her hair, bringing her lips to his.

The heat was instant, as always. It chased all traces of cold away.

"I thought I'd lost you tonight," he murmured against her mouth.

"I had the same fear when I couldn't get you to wake up in the car," she responded, her lips never moving away from his.

There was no more talking. Neither of them wanted to think about death. Not right now. Liam didn't want to even think about whether this was a good idea or not.

All he wanted to think about was her body pressed up against his.

ARMORED ATTRACTION

Janie Crouch

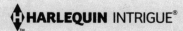

To my parents, for being a constant example of God's goodness,
faith and love. Thank you for being a blessing not only to me
but so many others.

Recycling programs
for this product may
not exist in your area.

ISBN-13: 978-0-373-74964-5

Armored Attraction

Copyright © 2016 by Janie Crouch

Printed in U.S.A.

HARLEQUIN®
www.Harlequin.com

Janie Crouch has loved to read romance her whole life. She cut her teeth on Harlequin Romance novels as a preteen, then moved on to a passion for romantic suspense as an adult. Janie lives with her husband and four children overseas. Janie enjoys traveling, long-distance running, movie-watching, knitting and adventure/obstacle racing. You can find out more about her at janiecrouch.com.

Books by Janie Crouch

Omega Sector: Critical Response

Special Forces Savior
Fully Committed
Armored Attraction

Omega Sector

Infiltration
Countermeasures
Untraceable
Leverage

Harlequin Intrigue

Primal Instinct

CAST OF CHARACTERS

Liam Goetz—Leader of the Omega Sector Critical Response Division's hostage rescue unit. Served in the army's Special Forces and in the Drug Enforcement Agency before coming to work for Omega Sector. Travels to the Outer Banks of North Carolina to help out an old flame he thought he'd never hear from again.

Vanessa Epperson—Social worker and former society princess of the Outer Banks. When she stumbles onto a human trafficking ring, she is forced to call the one man she's avoided—and kept an important secret from—for eight years.

Karine—Fifteen-year-old from Estonia in Eastern Europe. Victim of a human trafficking ring who escaped her captors.

Andrea Gordon—Behavioral analyst for Omega Sector's Critical Response Division, sent to help Liam, particularly with Karine.

Steve Drackett—Director of Omega Sector's Critical Response Division.

Derek Waterman—Tactical teams specialist for Omega Sector. Friends with Liam. Sent to help any way he is needed.

Joe Matarazzo—Hostage negotiator and part of the hostage rescue unit of Omega Sector. Friends with Liam and sent with Derek to help Liam with the case.

Marcus McBrien—Sheriff of the Nags Head police department.

Tommy Webb—Assistant sheriff of the Nags Head police department.

Chapter One

A leisurely walk along the beach in the evening was a chance for many people to ponder the meaning of life. Not for Vanessa Epperson. She rarely had time to walk along the beach at all anymore, much less waste that valuable time *pondering*.

She was way too busy to ponder. But, ahh, how she loved the feel of the sand on her toes.

She should have as much time as anyone to walk along the beach: her career as a social worker for a private organization—The Bridgespan Team—was technically nine to five, Monday through Friday. But in reality it rarely worked out that way. A call from a woman needing housing immediately because she'd finally gotten the courage to leave her abusive husband didn't always come during normal business hours. Nor did a call from someone who had his first critical job interview in weeks and needed a ride at 7:00 a.m. because his car had broken down.

Both of those scenarios had happened to Vanessa in the past forty-eight hours.

Her coworkers told her she got too involved, that she needed to keep more of a professional distance between herself and her clients. Vanessa just shrugged her colleagues off. Sometimes people needed help beyond what was required from the job. When she could help, she did. Because there were far too many times when there was just nothing she could do.

If they knew about it, she guessed most people would say she could dip into the five million dollars her parents had made readily available to her. But Vanessa couldn't do that. *Wouldn't* do that. She didn't plan to ever touch that money.

She pushed all thoughts of her family away as she walked along the sands of the Roanoke Sound of the Outer Banks of North Carolina. She wouldn't let them intrude on her rare moments of solitude and quiet.

But this sand—this particular sand—in her toes renewed her. Helped her to remember that everything would be okay. Helped her to clear her mind and leave the problems she couldn't solve somewhere else for a little while.

It was the beginning of October. The sun had set a few minutes ago, casting the beach in a purple hue. It was empty. With summer gone, most of the tourists had long since left the Outer Banks; they would've been on the ocean side anyway, rather than the more boring sound side. Most locals weren't out, either, having made their way to their homes or wherever they spent their evenings. Everyone was settling in.

Vanessa would need to do the same soon, too. Tomorrow's alarm at five thirty in the morning would come all too soon. She needed her sleep to fortify her for whatever the day would bring.

But since the beach was so quiet, the sand so nice and cool in her toes, the breeze so gentle in the ever-darkening sky, she decided to keep walking. She would just walk up to the beached log she could barely make out a couple hundred feet ahead, then turn around and go back to her car.

As with her family, she would categorically *not* think about other times she had walked along this very beach and whom she had walked along with. Thinking about it never led to anything but sadness anyway. Vanessa refused to be sad all the time. Life was too short.

Before she knew it she had made it to the log and was about to turn to walk back—until the log groaned and began to move.

Vanessa shrieked before she could help herself and jumped back. It was a *person*.

She looked around for any other people—aware after the past few years at her job that danger could be found in the most innocent-looking places—and grabbed her pepper spray from her bag. A gun would've been better—she was licensed to carry a concealed weapon in North Carolina—but hers was back at her car.

The log moaned again.

Vanessa worked her way closer, cautiously, running scenarios in her head. It could be a drunk person who had passed out on the beach. Didn't usually happen here, but it was possible. It could be someone who had fallen asleep.

It could be someone waiting to ambush her, although a mugging on the beach in October at this time of night was not very likely. Still, Vanessa kept her pepper spray close.

"Excuse me, are you okay?" When there was no answer she took a step closer. "Hello?"

Maybe it was someone hurt. She didn't let her guard down, but walked a few steps closer. Now she could see more of the person's shape.

If this person meant Vanessa harm, he or she must have a weapon. Now that Vanessa could see more clearly, she realized how small the person really was. Couldn't be much taller than Vanessa's own five feet two inches.

"Are you okay? Hello?"

Vanessa walked the rest of the way to the form. It was a female. She was lying unconscious on her stomach, long brown hair strung down her back, wet and full of sand and seaweed.

Vanessa reached down and pressed gently on the woman's shoulder. Her skin was icy to the touch.

Whoever this was needed help.

"Hello? Can you wake up?"

She could possibly have a head or spinal injury. Vanessa didn't want to move her. She cursed the fact that her cell phone was back in her car, although even if it was here, she probably wouldn't get a signal.

Vanessa rubbed up and down on the woman's arm. "Hello? Can you hear me?"

Vanessa jumped back when the woman suddenly scurried away from Vanessa's touch, chest heaving, breaths sawing in and out. She put an arm out in front of her in a defensive posture.

Not a woman. A girl. A teenager. Maybe fourteen or fifteen years old.

Vanessa's heart broke. She knew what that arm held out meant: abuse.

At least there didn't seem to be any spinal injury to worry about.

"Hi, I'm Vanessa." She spoke very slowly, softly. "Are you okay? How can I help you?"

Vanessa made no move to get any closer to the girl, not wanting to scare her further.

The girl shook her head, not saying anything.

Vanessa realized the girl was wearing a dark T-shirt that was ripped and falling off her body. She didn't seem to have anything on under it. Vanessa began to unbutton the lightweight jacket she was wearing.

"I'm just going to take off my jacket. You might feel a little better if you have on more clothes."

Vanessa worked it the rest of the way off then stretched out her arm and dropped it. It landed close enough for the girl to grab, but not so close that it would touch her if she didn't want it.

"Is there anyone I can call for you? Parents? Friend? Boyfriend?"

Vanessa was relieved when the girl reached for the jacket, but she didn't answer any of her questions.

"Can you at least tell me your name?"

The girl looked up at her, big brown eyes seeming to swallow her entire face.

"Ka-Karine," she finally whispered. "My name is Karine."

Her English was broken at best, heavily accented—sounding Eastern European. That was probably why she hadn't answered Vanessa's other questions. She didn't know enough English to understand what Vanessa was saying.

And unless she had family visiting here, she was also a long way from home.

"Hi, Karine," Vanessa said gently, slowing her speech significantly to see if it would help the girl understand any better. "Can you tell me how you got here?"

"Boat," Karine whispered.

"You were traveling on a boat? With your family? Was there an accident?"

Karine began to cry. "No. Men took us. Put us on boat for many days."

"Someone kidnapped you? From here in the Outer Banks?"

Vanessa could tell she had lost Karine again.

"Where are you from?" Slowly again. "Where is your home?"

"Estonia."

Vanessa wasn't sure where that was. The United States? An entirely different country?

"Is Estonia here in the United States?" Vanessa asked.

"No, it is near Russia."

Vanessa's breath whistled through her teeth. Was she understanding correctly?

"Some men came and took you from Estonia and put you on a boat?"

Karine nodded. "First one boat and then the smaller boat with the men who spoke only English."

Vanessa could see the girl begin to visibly shudder at the thought.

"And there were other girls with you?"

Karine nodded again. "Yes. There are seven more."

Vanessa felt nausea roll through her stomach. Karine and the other girls were obviously part of a human-trafficking ring right here in the Outer Banks.

"How did you get here, Karine?" Vanessa asked. "How did you get away from the men?"

She held up a hand covered in bruises around her wrist, obviously from handcuffs or other restraints.

"Man tie us when no one is on boat with us. But I got out. And then I jump in water. I rather die from sharks than let them touch me again." Karine closed her eyes and lowered her hand.

There weren't any sharks in the Roanoke Sound, Vanessa knew, although there could be painful jellyfish at this time of year. Either way, it had been an amazing feat for the small teenager to undertake. The Sound was more than five miles wide at some parts. There was no way Karine could've known how far she would have to swim when she'd jumped in.

Whatever had been waiting for her on that boat had to have been bad enough that Karine was willing to risk her life to get away from it.

Vanessa needed to get the girl to a hospital. Report this to the authorities. Get the cops or National Guard or Marines or all three to start looking for those other girls.

"Karine, you were so brave," she whispered. "I know it is hard, but do you think you could come with me? I can take you to the hospital. Get you the help you need."

"I promised other girls I would help them if I lived," Karine whispered.

"Yes." Vanessa nodded. "Absolutely. We will go to the police so they can help find the other girls."

Vanessa thought for a moment that Karine

might refuse her help, but she finally nodded and got up off the ground, wrapped in Vanessa's jacket.

"Okay, I go with you."

Karine didn't seem to have many significant injuries. She was able to walk unassisted from the beach to Vanessa's car. Dehydration was obviously an issue—she gulped down the contents of the water bottle Vanessa offered in seconds—as was hunger. She made short work of a package of crackers. Vanessa wished she had more to offer. She gave Karine a pair of yoga pants to put on, which were too big for the girl but at least were better than nothing.

Vanessa took a direct route to the Nags Head Regional Hospital. She'd brought in enough clients over the years that she was pretty well known there. She walked Karine in through the emergency entrance, relieved to see her friend Judy working the desk.

"Hey, Judy." Vanessa spoke only loud enough that the other woman could hear her. The last thing Karine needed was the media circus that would come along with anyone finding out she had been part of a probable human-trafficking ring in the area. "I have an assault victim here. Doesn't speak much English. Probably also suffering from dehydration. She swam a long way to get away from the person or persons who were holding her against her will."

Judy shook her head and smiled softly at Karine. "I'm so sorry, honey. We'll help you." She turned to Vanessa. "It's crazy busy in here tonight. Can we put her in temp room one? Just until something else opens up. We won't do any exams there."

Temporary room one was at the front of the trauma unit. They rarely put assault victims there because it was so busy nearby and was only separated by curtains. Judy wouldn't put them there if she had another choice.

"Okay, sure. I'll take Karine in myself."

She led the girl into the room and helped her to sit. She seemed to stare blankly out the crack in the curtain.

Should Vanessa get her some food? She didn't want to leave Karine alone, but who knew when she'd last had a decent meal? Maybe Judy could get something for them.

A moment later Karine bounded out of the chair and backed away to the farthest point in the room. Her face was devoid of all color and her eyes were huge.

"Leave. Leave." The young woman was shuddering so hard that was all she could get out.

Vanessa had no idea what was going on. Why was Karine freaking out now when she had been so docile since they'd arrived? Vanessa looked out through the crack in the curtain to where Karine had been looking.

A uniformed member of the sheriff's department was talking to Judy at the main desk.

Had Vanessa misunderstood the whole situation? Was Karine running from the law?

She turned back to the young woman and found her slipping under the curtains of the room. Vanessa rushed over, stopping her gently.

"Karine. The policeman out there… Is he looking for you?"

Karine clutched at Vanessa. "Man. Man on boat."

"That man was on the boat?" A sheriff's deputy?

"No." Karine shook her head. "That clothes."

Not that particular guy, but someone wearing the same uniform. Dear God. Was Karine telling her that someone from the sheriff's office was part of a trafficking ring?

Vanessa stared at her for a few more moments. She had no idea exactly what was going on, but she was willing to give Karine the benefit of the doubt. If Vanessa was wrong, she'd deal with the consequences later.

"Okay, let's get you out of here."

They slipped under the curtain and were out of the hospital in a matter of minutes. Karine was still shuddering, glancing from side to side frantically, obviously searching for anyone who might be following. Vanessa put an arm around her, tentatively, to guide her through the parking lot to her car. Karine stiffened briefly before leaning into her.

Vanessa started the car and pulled to the edge of the parking lot. She didn't know which way to turn. If someone from the sheriff's office really was in on this, it wouldn't take long for them to figure out Karine was with her. She couldn't take Karine to her house. She needed to get her out of the area.

"Karine." Vanessa turned to the girl, who was sitting low in her seat so no one could see her. "I'm going to drive you to Norfolk, okay? It's a city about an hour and a half from here. There are police, FBI, who can help us."

"No!" Karine sat straighter in the seat. "I cannot leave. I must stay here to help the other girls. Must find them."

"Yes, we'll get help and then come back here."

"No!" Karine repeated, grabbing for the door handle. "I stay here."

"No, wait. Don't get out," Vanessa said.

Karine was exhausted, traumatized and injured. Vanessa prayed she had been mistaken about the police uniform. Many of the men in the sheriff's department Vanessa had known most of her life. She couldn't imagine they would be involved with the victimization of girls.

But she wasn't about to put Karine out on her own, no matter how unlikely the scenario may be.

"Okay, we'll stay here in Nags Head," Vanessa

told her, watching her visually relax. "We'll go to a hotel."

Karine nodded and eased lower into her seat.

If Karine was going to refuse to leave the area, Vanessa was going to need to see about someone coming here to help them. Contacting the local police was out of the question. She needed someone outside that circle, someone in federal law enforcement.

Liam Goetz.

He was DEA, which maybe didn't deal with trafficking directly, but at least she knew he wasn't local. He'd know how to help or tell her who to contact.

Of course, she hadn't talked to Liam in eight years. Didn't even know if he would be willing to talk to her now. But he was her best chance in this situation. She had to try.

Vanessa sped to her apartment to get his phone number, which was written on the back of a picture of the two of them. She should've thrown it away years ago but hadn't been able to make herself do it. Now she was glad she hadn't.

She grabbed a couple changes of clothes from her room, but nothing to make it look as though she wasn't there, then ran back out to the car. She had no doubt one of the first places the police would start looking for Karine was at Vanessa's apartment.

As she pulled away, she Bluetoothed the number on the back of the picture. She forced herself not to look at the much younger, more innocent version of herself in the photo. That girl was gone forever.

The phone rang twice before someone answered. "DEA call center."

"Um, yes, I'm trying to reach an agent. At least he used to be an agent." Vanessa wasn't sure exactly what she should say. Maybe Liam didn't even work for the DEA anymore. "He gave me this number."

"Please provide the name of the person you are trying to reach and I'll direct your call." The operator was briskly efficient.

"Liam Goetz." Vanessa had no idea what department he worked for or even what city.

"Please hold."

Vanessa drove toward some older hotels closer to Nags Head. They weren't very expensive, which was pretty much all Vanessa could offer Karine right now. Plus, the police were probably less likely to look for her there.

The longer Vanessa was on hold, the more convinced she became that this whole call to Liam was probably useless.

"Hello? You're trying to reach Liam Goetz?" A briskly efficient female voice this time.

"Yes. But I don't know which division he's in—"

"I'm going to connect you to his voice mailbox.

Please leave a detailed message. We will make sure he gets it."

Okay, so evidently he did still work for the DEA. That was good.

"Okay."

"Please hold. Leave a message when you hear the beep."

Vanessa was startled, caught off guard, a moment later when she heard the beep. There had been no outgoing message.

"Um, Liam, it's Vanessa. Vanessa Epperson."

How much should she tell him?

"I'm still living on the Outer Banks, but I'm actually staying at a hotel at the moment." She gave him the name and address of the hotel they'd just pulled up to. "I need your help. I have a situation here and believe local police might be involved, so I need federal law enforcement. If you could just point me in the right direction, I would really appreciate it. I wasn't sure who else I could trust. Just call if you can."

She was rambling, so she left him her number and then disconnected the call. She'd done all she could do there. She knew she needed to have a backup plan in case Liam didn't call her back. After all, the last thing she'd heard him say about her eight years ago was that she was a selfish, spoiled brat who didn't have it in her to care about another person.

Yeah, she definitely better have a backup plan in place.

Chapter Two

Liam listened to the voice-mail message for the umpteenth time.

Vanessa Epperson.

He could honestly say he'd never expected to hear her voice ever again. After all, she hadn't even cared enough to leave him a voice mail eight years ago when she'd decided he wasn't good enough to marry.

Or a letter. Or an email. Or a face-to-face explanation.

But evidently she'd gotten over her phone aversion. Good for her.

Liam played the message again.

She needed help and was contacting him because she thought he was still DEA. He hadn't been DEA for more than five years, since Omega Sector's Critical Response Division had recruited him to lead their hostage rescue team.

Fortunately for Vanessa, since Omega Sector

was made up of agents from multiple different law-enforcement agencies—FBI, Interpol, DEA... Hell, Liam had worked a mission with a damn Texas Ranger last month—her message had been recorded and immediately forwarded to him.

She didn't mention what sort of trouble she was in, just wanted Liam to drop everything and help her. Like how she'd always wanted everyone to drop everything to do what she wanted. Some things didn't change.

He listened to the message one more time.

Liam should call one of his many friends from the head DEA office in Atlanta and have them send someone to Nags Head. Or he might even know someone at the FBI field office in Norfolk he could call.

It was the logical thing to do; probably the most professional answer to this situation. He could have someone there handling Vanessa's problem in three or four hours.

But who was Liam kidding? He wasn't going to make those calls. He was already walking down the hall of the Critical Response Division's head-quarters to his boss's office.

He wasn't sure what he was going to tell Steve Drackett. Just that he needed some time off to help an old friend. God knew Liam had enough time off saved up.

He knocked on Steve's office door, his back

office door that led directly to Steve himself, rather than pass through the main office entrance guarded by Steve's four assistants.

Four young, attractive, quite competent and intelligent female assistants.

Liam knew them all, flirted shamelessly with them all. He'd spent so much time in the office with those women that Steve had threatened to fire him several times.

Not that Liam dated any of them—he knew better than to date anyone who might have his life in her hands—but at any given moment he'd be leaning on their desks chatting, and keeping them from their work.

Liam smiled. Steve's main office was one of his favorite places in the world to be.

But not today. Not right now. He could not go in there and flirt with those beautiful women with Vanessa's voice still filling his head.

Steve's door opened.

"Hey, Liam. Come on in." Steve said, still reading from a file in his hand as he returned to his desk. "I didn't even think you knew this door existed. Hell, I wasn't really sure you knew any offices existed outside those belonging to my assistants."

Derek Waterman and Joe Matarazzo—both Liam's colleagues and good friends—were sitting in chairs across from Steve's desk. They held similar files.

"Hey, Goetz," Derek murmured. Joe muttered something unintelligible without looking up from the file in his hand.

"I don't mean to interrupt, Steve," Liam said.

"It's no problem. What's on your mind?"

"I'm going to need a few personal days."

Now the guys looked up from their files. Liam was pretty sure he'd never taken personal days except to go on actual vacations planned well ahead of time.

"Everything okay?" Steve's concern was also evident.

"Yeah." Liam shrugged. "Everything's fine. I just have a friend who called needing some help back in the Outer Banks. My friend said this might be a little sticky with the locals so wanted some outside help."

"You grew up there, right? You haven't been home in a long time."

"Yeah, not since my grandmother died. Not much there for me."

Steve nodded. "Is your friend's trouble serious? Do we need to send in a team?"

"Nah. I'm sure I can handle it."

"What sort of trouble?"

Liam sighed. "To be honest, I'm not exactly sure. My friend called my old DEA contact number. They forwarded it to me."

"Has anybody else noticed Goetz's complete lack of pronoun usage?" Joe said, leaning back in his chair.

Damn it. This was about to become a thing.

"As a matter of fact, I did," Derek responded, grinning. "So are we to assume this *friend* is of the female variety?"

Liam realized he should've just mentioned that from the beginning. "Yes, she is."

"Um, Joe, do you ever recall Liam being shy about mentioning a female friend to us before?" Derek quipped.

Liam knew his reputation. He'd worked pretty hard at making sure everyone knew he was a ladies' man. Girl in every port. Shameless flirt.

At times he almost believed his own press. Because it was a hell of a lot easier to believe that he was some sort of modern-day Casanova than that he still pined over a woman who'd left him cold eight years ago.

"A female from his hometown, no less," Joe responded. "I've never heard him mention any such creature before."

"Very curious, indeed." Derek waggled his eyebrows.

"All right, enough, you two," Steve cut in. He turned to Liam. "Like I said, is there anything we need to know about your friend or her situation?"

"Not as far as I know," Liam said. "She didn't

provide much detail. If it looks like something I can't handle, I'll let you know."

"You're not going to call her first? Get more details?"

"No, I'm just going to go."

Thankfully none of the three men in the room pointed out what Liam already knew: dropping everything and traveling from Omega headquarters in Colorado Springs to the Outer Banks of North Carolina because of a vague phone call from someone he hadn't talked to in nearly a decade was overkill.

But from the first moment he had heard Vanessa's voice, figured out she was asking for help, Liam knew he would be doing just that.

"Okay, I think one of the Omega jets is heading out to DC in the next few hours if you want to catch a ride there," Steve responded. "Be safe and keep me posted as to when you'll be back."

Joe and Derek didn't say anything, although they were both staring at Liam with mouths slightly agape. Liam ignored them.

"Okay. Thanks, Steve."

Liam just left. He didn't want to explain himself to his friends, especially when he could hardly understand what he was doing himself. All he knew was that he had to see Vanessa.

He wasn't really surprised that she was still living in the Outer Banks. The two-hundred-mile stretch of land, a string of barrier islands running along the northeast coast of North Carolina, held a great deal of prime property and the Eppersons owned a good chunk of it.

And Vanessa was princess of it all. She had been her whole life.

Liam had found out the hard way that her love for her pampered way of life outweighed any promises she might make to any poor sap fool enough to fall in love with her. Fool enough to believe her when she said she loved him, too.

Did she think of him when she felt the sand of the Roanoke Sound on her feet? On her back? Think of all the many hours they'd spent there together?

Did she ever think about him asking her to run away and marry him right there in that sand? About saying yes?

About not showing up where they were supposed to meet? About refusing to talk to him at all when he'd come by to see why she had changed her mind?

Probably not.

The address she had given him in the message was not her family mansion in Duck, which was slightly north of Nags Head and the preferred location for million-dollar mansions. It was some hotel he didn't recognize at Mile Marker 13, pretty much in the middle of nowhere.

Liam drove to his apartment and packed his things. He'd try to catch a ride with the team going to DC as Steve suggested. If not, he'd drive to Fort Carson, the army base in Colorado Springs. Omega worked pretty closely with the military when needed, and Liam had lots of contacts there from his days in Special Forces.

The commanding officers might lock their daughters away when Liam was in sight, but they would gladly welcome him on board an aircraft to give him a lift wherever he was going.

The thought brought a quick smile to Liam's face. His playboy reputation was well deserved. He'd certainly earned it since he'd been in Colorado.

Except for the past couple of years when he seemed to have lost his taste for fun, fast hookups. Yeah, he still flirted with all the gals—young or old—and kissed just about every woman he came across. But he wasn't particularly interested in more than that.

The thought of pseudo intimacy with another woman whose face he'd fondly remember but name he'd probably forget? Not as interesting anymore.

Maybe it had something to do with watching two of his best friends—and fellow Omega agents—fall in love with strong, beautiful women over the past few months. Jon Hatton and Derek Waterman's love for the women in their lives was downright palpable. Liam wanted something authentic like that for himself.

Then it struck him. *That* was why he was going to Nags Head. Because until he could put what had happened there behind him, he was never going to be able to have something real with any woman.

It was time. He was going to lay the ghost of Vanessa Epperson to rest once and for all. Her call was finally the excuse he needed.

LIAM WASN'T GOING to call.

Vanessa had accepted that reality when she woke up this morning, sleeping in a pretty dingy hotel, a traumatized teenager curled into the tightest of balls in the bed next to her. He'd had all evening, all night and some of this morning to respond, but hadn't.

Maybe he hadn't gotten the message. Maybe he was off on some important mission with the DEA or something.

Maybe he still hated her.

The reasons why he wasn't contacting her didn't really matter. All that mattered was that Vanessa was on her own in helping Karine.

That was okay. Vanessa had learned in the hardest way possible that she was capable of handling *on her own* almost anything that came her way. This situation was no different.

But Liam's lack of contact still stung a little bit.

She dragged herself out of bed, careful not to wake Karine. She knew from the girl's whimpers and cries throughout the night that she couldn't have gotten very good rest.

Karine needed help. Probably medical and definitely psychological—both more than Vanessa could provide. If the hospital and police weren't safe around here, then Vanessa was going to have to talk her into leaving the Outer Banks, at least for the day.

Vanessa poured water into the cheap four-cup coffeemaker on the bathroom vanity. Once she had coffee, no matter how bad it was, she'd be able to figure out a plan.

While she waited she turned on the local morning news. Although she doubted it, she was curious to see if there was any mention of Karine.

At first nothing, just weather and tides—an important part of life on a string of islands. But then the breaking news...

The sheriff's office had set up roadblocks at the bridges on both sides of Nags Head. They were looking for a federal fugitive—considered armed and very dangerous—and were stopping all cars leaving the island to search them.

Since there was only one road leading off Nags Head at the north and south bridges, she knew the police could, in essence, search every car attempting to leave the island.

The rest of the news report was about the traffic havoc the car-by-car search was creating.

No one from the sheriff's office seemed willing to comment.

Vanessa turned the television to mute and just stared at the screen.

Dangerous federal fugitive, her ass. Vanessa was one hundred percent certain the "dangerous federal fugitive" was curled up on the bed whimpering in her sleep every few minutes. But it meant that it would be impossible to get Karine off the island, at least today.

Not to mention that it confirmed that someone, at least one person pretty high up in the sheriff's department, was definitely a part of what had happened to Karine and the other girls.

The thought made Vanessa downright sick.

She grabbed her coffee, looking around. They weren't going to be able to stay here all day. They would need food—God only knew when Karine had last had a decent meal—and some other supplies. She'd given the girl a pair of shorts and a T-shirt she'd grabbed from her house, but they were too big.

She couldn't leave Karine alone while she went to get food, so she'd have to wait until she woke.

Vanessa needed to come up with a plan pretty darn quickly. But right now her options were limited.

A soft tap at the door startled her. She rushed to it but didn't say anything. She put her ear against the door. Maybe whoever it was—housekeeping?—would go away. She'd put the do-not-disturb placard on the doorknob.

"Vanessa, it's Liam. Open the door."

Chapter Three

Liam tapped on the door softly again. He was almost positive he had the wrong place. This was the address of the hotel Vanessa had mentioned on the voice mail, but this could not possibly be right.

Was it some sort of trap? Liam pulled his weapon from the belt holster attached to his jeans, but kept it low to his side. Had one of his enemies—and he had made plenty of them over the years—found out about his past with Vanessa and planned to use her against him in some way?

Because if that was someone's intent, it had succeeded brilliantly. Here Liam was, completely out in the open, at every possible tactical disadvantage, all because Vanessa had called.

But his history with Vanessa was long ago and buried pretty deeply. He hadn't even told his best friends about what had gone down between them. So he didn't really think there was any devious master plan, such as someone forcing her to make a phone call against her will.

But he still didn't put his weapon away. There was no way in hell Vanessa Epperson would be staying at a hotel like this if she had any other choice.

You really couldn't call it a hotel. It was more of a run-down motel, with all room doors leading directly outside to a parking lot that desperately needed repaving. There was no room service, spa or concierge.

Ergo—and obviously he'd been hanging around too many overthinking profilers at Omega if he was using words like *ergo*—no Vanessa.

He must be at the wrong place. He eased his weapon back into the holster and was turning to leave, not wanting to disturb whatever non-Vanessa person was sleeping in the room, when the door cracked open just the slightest bit.

"Liam?"

It was her. He couldn't see her through the crack, but he would know her voice anywhere, even if he hadn't heard it in her message recently.

"Yes. Are you okay? Let me in?" He took his weapon out again.

For a minute he didn't think she was going to do it, but then she stepped back and opened the door far enough for him to enter.

"What are you doing here?" she whispered. The

room was dark because of the pulled shades and he could hardly see her.

Liam looked around but didn't see anyone else that could be threatening Vanessa in the darkened room. He reholstered his weapon. "What do you mean, what am I doing here? You called me, needing help. That's what I'm doing here."

"Oh," she whispered again. "I thought you'd just call me back and leave me the contact info of someone in the DEA or something similar. Were you in the area?"

"Something like that." Absolutely nothing like that. "Why are we whispering?"

Vanessa turned and pointed over her shoulder. "Her."

There was a very small person balled up on the bed.

Okay. *This* was definitely not what he'd expected. The dumpy hotel. The hiding. The kid sleeping in the bed. "Vanessa, what the hell is going on?"

She shushed him with her finger then grabbed his arm, pulling him into the bathroom and closing the door behind her.

Now he could see her.

He refused to let his breath be stolen just because he was seeing her again for the first time in eight years. But damn if he could stop himself from staring at her.

Her hair was shorter now. Stopping just past her

shoulders rather than flowing down to nearly her waist as it once had. But it was still that same deep auburn color that reminded him of fall leaves or russet chrysanthemums. Her eyes were the same soft brown—although she had often worn colored contacts when she was a teenager, always wanting to be more *dramatic*. That had never made sense to Liam. Her eyes were stunning just the way they were.

She was still tiny. God, he'd forgotten how little she was. Her personality was so big, people tended to forget that she was barely five foot two and couldn't weigh more than a hundred pounds. Standing beside her now, Liam towered over her. As always, it didn't intimidate Vanessa.

Something was different about her now. He couldn't quite put his finger on it exactly, but something about her had changed.

Of course she was more mature, in her looks, even in her movements. But it was more than just that. Something in her eyes was different—a depth that hadn't been there before.

A depth that was only caused by living through pain. *Real* pain.

He knew that look, had seen it often enough when he served in Afghanistan with other men who had known heavy loss. A pain that would never be fully erased.

Liam couldn't even reconcile seeing a look like that on Vanessa. It just wasn't possible. He had known her since she was fifteen years old. Knew firsthand how selfish and self-centered she was.

So he had to be wrong about whatever he thought he saw in her eyes now.

"That girl out there is what the hell is going on," she said.

Liam had been so deep in his own thoughts he had forgotten he'd even asked the question.

"Who is she?"

"Her name is Karine. That's all she's told me so far. I found her when I was walking the Sound yesterday evening." Her eyes shot away from his as she said the words. "She was unconscious on the ground, in only a T-shirt. A teenager."

"Runaway?"

Vanessa cracked open the door so she could check on the girl and then closed it again. "No. I think she was part of a human-trafficking ring, Liam. She's from Eastern Europe somewhere— Estonia, I think she said—and was being held on a boat. Says there are other girls. Seven of them."

Liam muttered a curse under his breath. Human trafficking had been a huge issue up and down the entire east coast for years. He wasn't surprised to hear something had popped up in the Outer Banks. The string of islands was an ideal place to bring in a boat unnoticed. Easy access and tourists year-round, so locals wouldn't pay particular attention to a boat they didn't recognize.

What Liam didn't understand was why Vanessa

felt local law enforcement might already be aware or even a part of the situation.

"Explain more why you don't want to go to the local police. They would be best equipped to handle this, or at least begin the investigation. Have the most knowledge of the area."

Vanessa shrugged. "I'll admit I may be wrong about this. But I took Karine to the hospital yesterday evening so she could get checked out. She seemed to be keeping it together pretty well until she saw a sheriff's deputy at the nurses' station. She freaked out, Liam. Completely panicked." She touched his arm as she said it, then immediately dropped her hand again as if burned. "Sorry."

Liam had no idea what to say about her touch, so he just ignored it. "Did you press her about it?"

"Yes. It wasn't that particular officer she recognized, but she was convinced it was someone wearing that uniform."

The sheriff's uniform hadn't changed in the years that Liam was gone from the Outer Banks. It was still brown; still ugly. But it wasn't the only ugly brown uniform in the area—Liam hated to think they were suspicious of law enforcement when it could actually be a package delivery guy who was the perpetrator. A traumatized girl could easily be forgiven confusing two brown uniforms.

"There are a lot of brown uniforms out there," Liam said.

"I know. And I'm trying to keep that in mind.

But she was *convinced*. And I thought it was better to be wrong and have to apologize than her be right and back in her captors' clutches." She shrugged. "So we snuck out of the hospital without anyone seeing us."

He couldn't disagree with that line of reasoning. Under similar circumstances he probably would have done the same.

"The clincher for me was when I woke up this morning and there was a 'fugitive alert' and the police were checking cars trying to leave Nags Head." She shook her head. "I tried to take Karine to Norfolk last night, but she refused to go. Says she has to stay and help the other girls."

"She sounds like quite a kid," Liam said. "Strong."

"Yeah, but she needs help. I can't keep her cooped up in this hotel room. She needs a doctor and a counselor."

"I was wondering about this place. Why are you here? If you were trying to pick a place no one would ever search for Princess Vanessa, you certainly found it."

Her eyes narrowed. *Princess Vanessa* obviously still struck a nerve.

Her voice was tight. "I couldn't take her back to my place. And, yeah, I didn't want anyone to find me."

Liam had never been afraid to poke the tiger.

"Your dad would probably not be interested in a teenage misfit staying in the Epperson mansion."

She turned all the way from him then, in the guise of cracking the door to check on Karine again, but he could tell the topic didn't sit well with her.

"I don't live in my parents' house on Duck any longer, so I wouldn't take her there anyway. But, yes, I'm sure my dad wouldn't like it."

Duck, despite its corny name, consisted of mostly million-dollar mansions rather than the much less expensive vacation rentals, restaurants, and putt-putt golf places of the other islands in the Outer Banks.

Elitist in a word.

He shouldn't be surprised that she didn't live at home any longer. She was twenty-eight, for heaven's sake. No one would still live with their parents at that age if they had other options. Especially if Daddy paid for those other options, of which Liam had no doubt.

"So, where's your place?"

"In Kitty Hawk."

He raised an eyebrow. "On the beach?"

"No."

"On the Sound, then?" She had to live on the water. Vanessa Epperson had always lived on the water.

"Look, where I live is not important, okay? I just couldn't chance taking her to my place. Not if the police are after her and someone at the hospital reports she's with me."

He could agree that Vanessa's suspicions of the police were grounded, given Karine's fear of the uniform and the car-search tactics this morning. Until they knew for sure, they would keep all actions under wraps.

"Why don't I go in to the sheriff's office today and feel things out? I could tell them I'm here on vacation or something."

Her eyebrow rose. "You really think they're going to talk to you at all? You have a history with the Outer Banks police. They probably haven't forgotten that."

It was true. Liam had been a hell-raiser back in his juvie days. His grandmother had done the best she could with the wild child she'd been forced to raise after both his parents had died suddenly when he was ten. But even her loving yet strict hand hadn't been enough to keep him out of pretty regular trouble with the law when he was a teenager. Nothing too serious: some fights, occasional vandalism, a few nights of disturbing the peace after he'd been able to talk some poor tourist into buying him alcohol.

He was actually thankful for a lot of his misspent youth. During one of the times the sheriff's office had handcuffed him to a chair, he'd met Quint Davis, the DEA agent who had taken the time to look past Liam's rather gruff exterior and talk to the half boy, half man underneath.

Quint had gotten Liam to join the army and then picked him up as a DEA agent immediately after Liam's discharge, which had eventually led to his job at Omega. Liam owed the man his life.

But, yeah, anybody who had worked at the Outer Banks sheriff's office for more than ten years was going to remember him. He doubted they would even know he was law enforcement now, unless they ran a background check on him.

"Well, this time I'm not some kid they've arrested for stumbling drunk down the beach."

Their eyes locked. He had met Vanessa on just such an occasion. She had stuck her snooty little nose up at him and told him to go find a bench and sleep it off.

He hadn't been able to help falling in love with her right then and there.

"I'll just be checking in as a professional courtesy, as a fellow law-enforcement officer," Liam continued, ignoring the shared memory between them. "When I heard about the escaped fugitive, I wanted to see if there was anything I could do to help."

Vanessa was nodding, about to respond, when they heard a cry from the bedroom.

"Miss Vanessa?" The voice was lost. Sorrowful. Frightened.

Vanessa ran to the young girl, but Liam kept

his distance. He had no doubt she would not want to be near a man right now.

"I'm here, Karine. I was just in the bathroom."

Karine all but jumped into Vanessa's arms.

Vanessa sat on the bed and smoothed the girl's hair, holding her loosely so she wouldn't feel trapped.

"Who is that man?" Karine asked.

"He's my friend. His name is Liam. He's going to help us get you and the other girls to safety."

Karine reached over and turned on the lamp next to the bed. Liam just stood there as she watched him with eyes that had seen too much. Even if they got this girl to safety today, away from the horror she had lived through, she would never have a child's innocence again.

Her childhood had been finished from the moment someone had kidnapped her and thrown her on a boat.

Finally she nodded. "Okay," she said to Vanessa.

Liam guessed he'd passed the test.

They needed a plan. But first Liam knew that everyone needed food.

"I'll go grab some breakfast from—"

His words were interrupted by a pounding on the door.

"This is the Outer Banks Sheriff's Department. Open the door."

Chapter Four

Vanessa stood. The sheriff's department had found her? How? She hadn't used a credit card.

This was the problem with living in a relatively small town. There were no secrets. One call from the police to the front desk in a systematic search and the clerk would undoubtedly have remembered her and told them. It was pretty odd for Vanessa to be at a hotel of this caliber, since most people knew her face and reputation—the Outer Banks princess—but didn't really know anything about her. They assumed she still lived off her parents' money, just as Liam had assumed in the bathroom.

She didn't. She hadn't for more than eight years.

It really didn't matter how the officer had found her. She had to figure out what to do.

They couldn't get out the one window of the room; it was right next to the door. There was no window in the bathroom, either.

The pounding on the door came again. Not obnoxiously loud, but firm enough to know whoever was on the other side meant business. "I need to speak with Vanessa Epperson."

Tears were running down Karine's face but she made no sound. Vanessa glanced frantically around the room before her gaze settled on Liam.

Who was taking his shirt off?

"Get her into the bathroom, then come back out here." He looked at Karine. "Stay very quiet in there. We'll take care of this."

The young girl nodded and ran to the bathroom. As soon as she turned away, Liam kicked off his shoes and socks and started unbuttoning his jeans, before pulling them, and his underwear, all the way off.

Liam was naked.

Vanessa pulled the bathroom door closed behind her and tried not to stare but could not help herself.

Liam was *naked*.

He ruffled his own hair so it stood on end, then turned and walked to the door, opening it a few inches.

"Man, what is going on? Do you know what time it is?" Liam looked down at an arm that didn't have a watch on it. "Neither do I. But it's like the butt crack of dawn."

"Um, excuse me, sir."

Vanessa couldn't see the officer but could hear the discomfiture in his voice.

"We were told that Vanessa Epperson was staying in this room."

"Well, she is, man." Liam yawned and ran a hand through his hair. "But she's a little worn out right now if you know what I mean."

Liam opened the door a little farther, his nakedness causing the man to step back rather than step closer to look inside.

"Um, could you put some clothes on, sir? I'd like to talk to Miss Epperson, please."

The officer wasn't going to be deterred, although Liam was doing his best. Vanessa wasn't sure if the officer could enter the room without a warrant, since it was a hotel, not a home, but she didn't want to find out.

She pulled off her pajamas—T-shirt and shorts—so she was also naked, grabbed the sheet off the bed and wrapped it around herself. She wasn't as bold as Liam and willing to answer the door buck-naked.

"Hey, baby." She walked up behind Liam and slid her arms around his chest, running them over his pecs and abs, feeling them tighten under her fingers. "What's going on?"

This is all just an act. This is all just an act. This is all just an act.

Liam put an arm around her and pulled her in

front of him so the sheet was covering them both from the officer outside.

But her very naked back was pressed to his very naked front. *All* of his naked front. Vanessa couldn't stop the shiver that ran through her entire body when he reached down and kissed the tender skin joining her neck and shoulder.

This is all just an act.

"This officer of the law was looking for you," Liam said in that friendly mocking voice only he seemed to be able to pull off without offending people. "Have you been a naughty girl?"

Vanessa could tell the more intimate she and Liam pretended to be, the more uncomfortable the young officer became. She turned partway in Liam's arms so she was half facing him. "What if I have?"

He leaned down and kissed her, biting her lip with his teeth and pulling on it before letting it go. "Well, I'd have to do something about that, wouldn't I?" He nipped at her lip again. "First I'd have to—"

The officer cleared his throat in an embarrassingly loud manner, stopping whatever scene Liam was about to describe.

This is all just an act. This is all—

"Excuse me, sir…ma'am. I'm Officer Atwood. I just have a few questions. Then I'll let you get back to your…business."

Vanessa kept the sheet clutched at her chest, making sure it didn't fall too low. But she could feel Liam's hands on her waist, rubbing tiny little circles with his fingers. Moving down to her hips and back up again. The feeling was delicious. She wanted to push his hands away but couldn't if she didn't want to give the officer of the law a peep show.

Liam pulled her back, flush against his body. Vanessa barely kept in the moan that wanted to escape her.

This was all just an act.

"Yes, Officer Atwood. What's your question?"

Evidently the act was working, because the poor officer standing in front of her didn't know where to look and barely seemed to know how to pose his question.

"Um, last night, did you have a teenage girl with you?"

Liam's fingers stopped their rubbing and gripped her hips tightly in warning. She knew she couldn't totally deny being with Karine. Obviously the sheriff's department already knew that, had probably been told that by Judy at the hospital. There wouldn't be any reason for her not to tell them.

"Yeah, that runaway kid? Bless her heart. She was not looking so good. I picked her up off Highway 158. We went by 7-Eleven to get some food—

I don't trust runaways with cash, it's often used to immediately buy drugs—and then I took her to the hospital, since it looked like she might have some injuries or something."

Liam's fingers resumed their circles.

"Did she tell you her name, where she was from?"

Vanessa shook her head. "Katy or something, I think? She didn't really talk much at all. I think she might have been on something. Why? Did she do something bad after I left her at the hospital?"

"You just left a minor at the hospital? Don't you work in social services, Miss Epperson?"

Uh-oh. The officer was right. Vanessa would never have left a teenager alone at the hospital. She felt Liam's fingers tighten again.

"Yeah, but I'm not a social worker around the clock." She smiled at the officer. "It was after eight. I had other plans that very definitely did not involve a teenage girl." Vanessa allowed herself to melt back into Liam. He pulled his hand up from her waist to tilt her head back against his shoulder so he could kiss her.

She was instantly thrown back into old times. The heat between them had always been almost palpable. They might have yelled at each other, fought and wanted to kill each other at times, but whenever they had been this close, an undeniable passion had flared between them.

Vanessa couldn't help herself; she twisted, trying to get closer to him.

Until she heard the officer clear his throat once more.

Damn it. *This is all just an act.* Remember that.

Liam brought his lips up from hers. "*I* was her other plans," he said to the officer, winking, deliberately downplaying his intelligence. Anything to keep the other man's guard down.

It worked. Atwood rolled his eyes. "Yeah, I got that. Thanks." He looked at Vanessa. "So you left the girl at the hospital?"

"I checked her in with one of the nurses, asked her to call social services—you know, someone who was actually on the clock—and pretty much left. Because, like I said…other plans."

"And you didn't have her with you for the rest of the night?"

One of Liam's arms came to rest across her chest, hooking around the top of her opposite shoulder, pulling her farther back against him. "Officer, if we had a kid in the room with us while doing some of the stuff we did last night, you would have to arrest us right now." He winked again.

"Hey!" Vanessa feigned outrage and elbowed him in the stomach. Or rock-hard abs.

"Sorry, baby," he whispered, "but you know it's true."

"Is the girl in some sort of trouble?" she asked Atwood.

"She's a suspect in some burglaries of homes in the area, so we're trying to find her."

"Darn it. I was hoping she was just a runaway who could be reunited with her parents. Some kids get away from home and when faced with the reality of the streets realize that home wasn't such a bad place, after all."

Officer Atwood shook his head. "She's definitely wanted by the police."

"Okay, well, if for some reason I see her again, I'll be sure to let you know."

Liam was starting to play with her bare shoulder with his fingers as though he was getting impatient for the officer to be gone.

"Okay. Thank you for your time. Sorry to have interrupted your...rest."

"No problem, man. I think we might go back inside and play out our own version of good cop, bad cop."

Vanessa giggled as Liam dragged her inside and shut the door.

"Do you think he bought—"

Her words were cut off by his mouth swooping down and devouring hers.

This time it was not just an act.

Vanessa gave herself over to the kiss, to the heat. As always, she didn't have any choice. It consumed her. The thin bed sheet was the only thing between them as he lifted her and pressed her against the door they'd just closed.

She couldn't hold back the moan. She didn't even try. She wrapped her fingers in his brown hair, still as silky and thick as she'd remembered it, and pulled him closer.

It was as if all the years they'd been apart melted away; all the pain they'd caused each other never happened.

Except it had. Both seemed to remember that at the same time.

And that they had a very scared teenager in the bathroom.

Liam eased back and Vanessa slid down the door until her feet were on the floor. She unwound her hand from his hair and grabbed the sheet that covered her again, since it was in danger of falling now that they were no longer pressed together.

"You okay?" he asked.

Was she okay? No, not by any stretch of the imagination was she okay. "Yeah, I'm fine."

He nodded then turned away to start dressing. She kept her back to him and did the same, in her clothes this time rather than her pajamas.

"I'm going to check on Karine," she said without looking at him. Vanessa wasn't sure she was ever going to be able to look at Liam again.

That was too bad, considering he was still just as ridiculously gorgeous as he had been eight years ago. Brown hair and green eyes. She had always been so damn jealous of those clear green eyes of his.

She tapped on the bathroom door and opened it a crack.

"Karine? It's safe now, honey."

She didn't hear anything so she opened the door farther. "Karine?"

She wasn't in the bathtub or behind the door. There was no window in the room for her to have climbed out.

"Miss Vanessa?" The sound came from the cabinet that ran under the length of the sink vanity.

Vanessa crouched and opened the cabinet. Oh, God, the girl had crammed herself in there to hide. It couldn't have been comfortable.

"Come on out, honey. It's safe now." She helped Karine unfold herself from her small hiding space.

"I want to make sure nobody find me."

"You did great, Karine." Vanessa wrapped her arms around her and pulled the girl close. Even though she was so young, she was almost the same height as Vanessa. "It was the perfect hiding spot, but you're safe now."

"I was scared."

"I don't blame you."

Liam turned from where he stood at the window. "Ladies, we can't stay here."

"Do you think that officer will come back?" Vanessa asked.

"Not him. I think we traumatized him enough.

But once he reports that he found you, Vanessa, but did not actually search the room, somebody else—higher up who won't be scared by a couple of naked people—will be coming back here. We need to get out now."

Vanessa took her arm from around Karine. "I'll go get your clothes so you can change, okay?"

She grabbed the same clothes from yesterday—yoga pants that were too large and another T-shirt—and walked them to Karine. She left the bathroom and closed the door behind her.

Liam was standing a few feet away directly in front of her. He folded his arms over his chest and she couldn't help noticing the bulge of his biceps. Liam had always been in good shape, even when they'd known each other before.

Now he was rock solid. Everywhere. This morning's theatrical performance had proved that.

It was totally unfair that he looked just as good in clothes as he did without them. And that she was still so *affected* by him.

"I think you owe me an explanation." The intensity of his voice caused parts of her deep inside to flutter.

"About what? I told you pretty much everything I know about Karine."

"Not about Karine. About you. What the hell is going on with *you*?"

Vanessa shrugged, confused. "I don't know what you mean."

"Well, let's start with the two words I never thought I'd hear used to describe you. *Social worker.*"

Chapter Five

Liam felt as if he were having an out-of-body experience.

To get rid of that young Deputy Atwood, he'd had to think fast. Sordid affair was the first thing that had come to his mind when he looked at this place, so he'd decided to play that angle.

He definitely hadn't expected Vanessa to jump in and help with the ruse when the officer wasn't buying it despite Liam's best efforts to make him so uncomfortable that he just went away. And her actions had made the difference.

Of course, the officer couldn't just barge in without a warrant—a hotel was considered a temporary home in the eyes of the law and most of the same rules applied—but if they refused him entry with no grounds whatsoever, Atwood would've been suspicious. He would've called it in and then the sheriff's department would've just waited them out. Sooner or later they'd have to leave and the hotel room only had one entrance and exit.

Sitting ducks.

So Vanessa's help in fooling the officer had just bought them some desperately needed time. Not much, but enough.

Vanessa's naked body pressed up against his naked body? That searing kiss that threatened to turn his bones to ash?

Yeah, out-of-body experience.

All of that was nothing compared to hearing the words *social worker* used to describe Vanessa Epperson's profession. There was no way the spoiled, selfish, but full-of-life woman he'd known eight years ago had become a social worker. Someone who took care of other people.

But he couldn't deny the tenderness she'd showed as she'd cared for Karine since he'd arrived. It was hard to reconcile the Vanessa gently holding a traumatized teenager with the Vanessa he'd known before.

There were pieces of the puzzle—many of them, it seemed—that he was missing. Some were obvious now that he was looking for them.

For example, what were these clothes she was wearing? A pair of non-designer, off-the-rack jeans and a simple green cotton T-shirt. Liam could very clearly remember her teaching him about silk, cashmere and Pashmina—by wrapping her naked body in each and making him guess—

scoffing that cotton shirts for women were only as a last resort.

Evidently, this situation was a last resort, then.

Her tennis shoes were no-name brand, also. He was pretty sure you could pick them up at the local supercenter.

Vanessa Epperson at the local supercenter?

Out-of-body experience.

She was looking at him now as if she didn't know quite where to start. And it didn't matter anyway, because they had to get out of there.

"You know what?" He cut her off as she began to speak just as Karine opened the bathroom door. "Save it. We've got to move."

He took a step closer. "But I will be told exactly what is going on."

Vanessa nodded.

Liam winked and smiled at Karine, not wanting her to think any tension between him and Vanessa should worry her. She smiled back at him, albeit timidly.

"I'm going to go drive around for about five minutes, see if we have anybody watching the room."

He pulled his cell phone out of his pocket and texted Vanessa so she would have his number.

"That's me." He nodded in the direction of her phone when it chirped. "You two be ready to go in case I have to come get you in a hurry."

He hoped it wouldn't come to that. Nags Head—

really none of the Outer Banks islands—wasn't big enough for them to escape in a high-speed chase with the police. Their best bet was to get out now while they could.

"Is your car hidden somewhere?" he asked Vanessa.

"No." She shook her head. "I didn't think I needed to. I didn't think they would be looking for me so fast."

"That car right out front is yours?" Liam couldn't keep the shock from his voice.

She nodded, eyebrow raised, as if daring him to say something further.

At sixteen she'd had a BMW. And now she was driving an early 2000s–model Camry? Not that there was anything wrong with a Camry: safe, dependable, known to last. If she'd had the latest model, he would've considered it a wise, mature choice.

But a model that was at least a dozen years old?

The out-of-body experiences just kept on coming.

"Okay, well, just be ready in case you need to drive it. Don't open the door or peek through the window until you hear from me in case someone is watching the room."

"Be careful," Vanessa said. Karine had come to stand right beside her and she slipped an arm around the girl.

"I will. Be ready."

Liam walked out the door, whistling and tossing his keys. If anyone was watching the room, he wanted it to look as if he was in no hurry, that he was just a happy, sated guy going to grab some coffee.

As he got to his car, which he'd parked toward the front of the lot away from Vanessa's, he missed the keys he was tossing on purpose so they fell to the ground. As he crouched to get them, he stayed down to fake tying his shoe, taking survey of the parking lot as he did so.

There were two other cars in the lot and both had been there before Liam arrived. One was near the front desk, probably the clerk's. The other was a few spots down from Vanessa's Camry, not an optimal place for surveillance, but not terrible.

Liam honestly didn't think they were watching the hotel yet. No doubt they would be soon after the officer made his report. Liam was willing to bet the young officer probably didn't know the importance of what he had been tasked to do. He thought he was looking for someone who had last been seen with a teenage, petty burglar. He probably felt he'd drawn the short straw this morning and wouldn't be in any hurry to report questioning a naked guy that hadn't resulted in anything useful.

They needed to use that situation to their advantage.

Liam drove slowly out of the parking lot. There

were no cars around the streets with anyone sitting in them in stakeout fashion. Nor any vans that could be used for surveillance.

The hotel was clean.

He'd drive around for a few minutes just to make sure. See if anyone followed him. He also needed to figure out a larger game plan now that he was also convinced someone at the sheriff's office was in on the trafficking ring. Too much time was being placed on finding Karine for him to think otherwise.

He needed to find a safe place to stash both Karine and Vanessa. Nothing that was connected to Vanessa in any way. He knew just the place but he didn't know if Vanessa would like it.

Too bad.

After driving around the block twice, and turning around and driving a different block in another direction, Liam was sure no one was following him. He stopped at a doughnut shop for coffee and doughnuts, as one last precaution, and because they needed food anyway.

And Vanessa could not survive without coffee.

The thought popped into his head unbidden. But to be honest, Liam wasn't sure if that was true anymore. He had no idea what was true about Vanessa. He got her coffee anyway.

Right before he left the shop, he texted her to let him know he was coming. ETA five minutes.

Watch for me through the peephole and get out fast. Keep K's head covered.

This was it. Either the hotel was under surveillance or it wasn't. Regardless, now was when they were going to make their move.

Liam drove back to the hotel as if he wasn't in any particular hurry. Still no sign of any tail. The moment he pulled up to the hotel, the door to the room opened and Vanessa flew out, her arm around Karine, her jacket draped over the girl's head. She opened the back door to his SUV and they both piled into the backseat.

Liam was pulling out of the parking spot before Vanessa's door even closed.

This time he did not drive leisurely. He didn't drive fast enough to attract attention to them, but he got out of there with purpose.

The problem when trying to lose a tail in the Outer Banks was the lack of main roads. Highway 158 was the main four-lane drag, and that was about it. There was also Highway 12 that ran parallel to 158, but it was a two-lane and much slower. All Liam could do was take the back roads and cut-throughs that he remembered from his youth.

This wasn't his first time trying to get away from the Outer Banks police without calling attention to himself.

Vanessa and Karine kept crouched in the backseat so it would look as if Liam was driving alone. If they did happen to pass anyone studying the drivers of vehicles, they wouldn't be looking for him.

"Do you think anyone is following us?" Vanessa asked after a few minutes.

"No, I think we got out in time." If someone was following them, he'd know it by now. The winding route he'd taken over the past mile would've made it obvious.

"What about my car?"

"I think it's better to leave it there. Maybe it will buy us a few hours' time if they think we're still in the room. This car wasn't parked near you, so hopefully Officer Atwood didn't notice."

"Okay. What are we going to do? I'm sure they're still searching cars, right? We can't make it off the islands."

"No leave, Miss Vanessa," Karine said. "Must help other girls. *Must.*"

The girl didn't know a lot of English, but she knew what she wanted.

"It's okay, Karine." He glanced back at them in the rearview mirror. "We're not leaving. We want to help them, too."

"Can you call your DEA contacts in, Liam?" Vanessa asked. "Or the FBI or whoever handles cases like this? Obviously we don't know who we can trust with the local police."

"I'm not actually with the DEA anymore. Haven't been for the past five years."

"But I left a message for you with the DEA. How did you get it if you don't work there?"

He glanced at her again. Confusion was evident on her face.

"I now work for an interagency task force called Omega Sector, in their Critical Response Division. I'm head of the hostage rescue team."

He watched as her eyes widened and her mouth fell open before turning his gaze back to the road.

"Sounds like you're pretty qualified to handle what's going on here, then. You have people you can call in? People with big guns who can shoot the bastards responsible for this?"

Liam rolled his eyes. "Generally we arrest the bad guys unless they shoot at us first, but, yes, I can get a whole team here."

"Then why haven't you done that yet? Those girls are somewhere out there, trapped. Hurt and desperate."

He glanced in the mirror again and saw Karine's face growing paler. He caught Vanessa's eye and gestured with his head toward Karine. Vanessa looked down at the girl and immediately slipped an arm around her.

"I'm sorry, sweetie. I shouldn't have said that."

"It's okay," Karine whispered. "They need help."

"And we will help them. We'll get Liam's friends here—people who help others all the time—and we'll get the other girls out."

Liam caught Vanessa's eye in the rearview mirror again. "We'll talk specifics later."

She nodded, tugging Karine closer.

"Where are we going right now?" Vanessa asked.

"We've got to get off the streets. Once they figure out we're not in the hotel, they'll start searching again. I'm going to take you somewhere not related to you at all."

"Another hotel?"

"No, that will always leave witnesses. A house."

She shook her head. "A friend's? Are you positive you can trust the person?"

"No. My grandmother's house. I still own it."

That silenced her.

He had a cleaning service come in once a month to clean, keep it in shape and take care of any repairs. He even paid for power and water each month, which wasn't much because it was so small.

After his grandmother died, he hadn't been able to sell it. He had said it was because she'd been his last living relative—the only roots he'd ever had—and he didn't want to part with it if he didn't have to. But he couldn't deny the other part of that truth now.

He'd kept the house because it was the first place he and Vanessa had made love.

Chapter Six

An hour later they were safely tucked away in Liam's grandmother's house. His house now.

They had stopped briefly at a grocery store, Vanessa and Karine tucked low in the backseat as Liam ran in. They had agreed it was better to go to the store now to get what they needed so they were prepared for as long as possible.

In the house of a million memories.

But Vanessa would accept living with the memories, as painful as some were, if it meant they were safe. If it meant Karine could get some real food and the real rest that she needed. If it meant they could figure out where the other girls were being held and do something about it.

She still didn't understand why Liam hadn't just called in the SWAT cavalry or whatever. But he had been right; they didn't need to talk about those details in front of Karine.

Liam had come back to the SUV in less than

fifteen minutes. He hadn't said anything as he opened the hatchback and put the grocery bags inside. Hadn't hurried around to the driver's side. Hadn't done anything that would call attention to himself.

He was good, Vanessa could definitely see that.

He hadn't talked until he was pulling out of the parking lot.

"You girls okay?" he asked.

"Yes. Any problems?"

"Nope. Got food and even a couple T-shirts and sweatpants. I had to get four different sizes, so I explained it was for my family while we're visiting."

"Because you buying a size extra-small pants and shirt might have been memorable."

"Exactly. All the cloak-and-dagger was probably unnecessary, but always better to be safe."

He *was* good. He'd thought of details Vanessa probably would've missed.

The drive to his grandmother's house—*his* house—took about twenty minutes. They had gone to a grocery store on the opposite side of Nags Head just in case someone remembered seeing him or his car.

But now they were inside, car pulled behind the back, Karine well fed and sleeping in one of the bedrooms.

"She still needs medical and psychological help. Professional help," Vanessa said. It was probably too late for any sort of assault kit to yield any results, but everything should still be documented.

"Yeah, those bruises on her wrists are pretty bad. And I hate to say this, but I'm sure she was assaulted, right?"

Vanessa rubbed a hand over her eyes. "She won't talk about any specifics, but, yes, I would say most definitely."

Liam reached out and pulled her down next to him on the seat at the table.

"She's a survivor," he said. "She's strong."

"I know. I just can't bear to think about what she's been through."

"We'll get her a counselor and a doctor. We just have to figure out who we can trust."

She nodded. "Why haven't you called in some sort of attack team yet?"

"Because if we send in a blitz attack on the sheriff's office, not knowing who exactly is involved and to what degree, the first thing the kidnappers will do is kill the remaining girls. They're liabilities."

Nausea pooled in Vanessa's stomach. "I hadn't thought of that. But you're right."

She rested her face in her hands.

"That doesn't mean we're not going to stop them, Nessa. It just means we're not going to roll in guns blazing."

He'd called her Nessa. He was the only one who

ever had, ever dared. She hadn't heard that name in eight years.

"Not to mention," he continued, "it's the word of one small foreign girl, supposedly wanted by the law, against the word of people who may have lived in this area their whole lives."

"But I know she's telling the truth," Vanessa said. She had no doubt about it at all.

Liam nodded. "I believe her, too, but it's about what we can prove when it comes down to a court of law."

"I just can't stand the thought of more girls trapped and scared." Karine had told them that the youngest of the girls was only eight years old. Fortunately she was being "kept" for someone special—some sick buyer, no doubt—so she hadn't been assaulted. The older girls hadn't been so lucky.

Liam reached over and grasped her hand. "I know. I feel the same. But it's important that we keep whoever is behind this in the dark as long as possible. That is our best chance at saving those girls. By convincing law enforcement that you don't really know anything about Karine and that you certainly don't know where she is now."

Vanessa nodded. He was right.

"Okay, then I need to call my office, let them know I won't be coming in. If I just don't show up, everyone there will be worried."

Vanessa stood and called her supervisor at Bridgespan. It wasn't a long conversation. Vanessa told her she was sick but that she would hopefully be in tomorrow. Her boss understood and told her to take care of herself.

"That seemed pretty painless," Liam said after she finished. He was sitting back in his chair, long legs stretched out in front of him, arms crossed over his chest.

He looked relaxed, lazy even, in that way Liam could pull off so well. But Vanessa had no delusions. He intended to have answers from her about the changes in her lifestyle.

She didn't want to fight with him. Didn't want to go back to eight years ago in some epic battle of "who was right and who was wrong when we were young and stupid." But she could at least give him the basics.

"You want answers."

"I would just like to know what is going on. I find I do better in any tactical situation when I know all the information."

Was that what she was? What they were? A *tactical situation*?

"There's not a whole lot to the story. I grew up. Decided I couldn't live on my parents' money forever."

"And became a social worker. Like with a degree and everything?"

She could tell he tried very hard to keep any trace of incredulity out of his voice, and almost succeeded.

It stung a little. But it was the most common sentiment among people who had known her then and knew her now. Why would Liam be different?

Vanessa ten years ago would never have been a social worker. An interior decorator? Maybe. Buyer for some fashion line or upscale boutique? Perhaps. Professional country club attendee and beach bunny? Absolutely.

Helping other people for barely over minimum wage? No.

But she wasn't that person anymore. Thank God, she wasn't that person anymore. Although the change had come at a high price.

"After you left...after..." She trailed off. She didn't want to talk about that. About him leaving or what had happened afterward. "I decided to go to college. I didn't want to just sit around here anymore. I really enjoyed my basic psychology and sociology classes, and so followed that route. Ended up with a degree in social services." In less than three years, she might add.

"Wow." He shook his head. "I just never would've figured—"

"That I would ever be anything but a selfish, spoiled brat who didn't have it in her to care about another person?"

Silence fell between them. That was the quote, almost word for word, that he'd told his friends about her when he left. After he'd asked her to come away with him and get married and she'd said yes but then hadn't.

For reasons he didn't understand. And, once she'd found out what he'd really thought about her, for reasons she'd had no plans to ever tell him.

"You made a promise and then broke it." Liam rubbed a hand over his face. "I was angry. Hurt. Plus, it was the truth." He sat straighter in his chair. "How did you find out I said that?"

"I went looking for you. Your friends were happy to relay the message." They'd never liked her. Had always thought she was a snob.

"When did you come looking for me?"

"Maybe a week after you left?"

"Why then?"

Because it was the first time she had been able to. But again, not telling him that. "I wanted to see if there was any chance you were still around."

That mocking smile, so fake and handsome— the one that had always gotten under her skin— covered his face now. "Why? Didn't think I'd actually leave? Even though you didn't even have enough guts to explain to me yourself that you were no longer interested in marrying me? I had to find out by knocking on your door and your father telling me?" He stood from the table and walked over to the sink, farther from her. "Nope. I left and never looked back."

This was the fight she'd been trying to avoid. It was a situation too many years past, water having long since washed under the bridge. Pride and stubbornness and tragedy conspiring together to keep them apart.

Vanessa turned and walked over to the window. This place was so bittersweet for her. Every time Liam's grandmother had gone off to the grocery store or her bridge club or, heaven forbid, a weekend trip up to Norfolk to see her cousin, Vanessa and Liam immediately jumped into his big bed. They'd never been able to get enough of each other. She was surprised they hadn't burned down the whole house with the passion between them.

Yeah, she'd been selfish and spoiled, but she'd loved Liam Goetz with every fiber of her being. Hearing that he'd said how selfish and undesirable she was—combined with everything else she'd gone through at that time—had cut her to the quick. Him walking away and never looking back? That had just proved to her that he hadn't loved her in the same way she had loved him.

It had caused her to do something she hadn't done in the entirety of her selfish, spoiled life.

Give up.

She should've fought for him. For them. But hadn't had the strength at the time.

So after she'd healed, she'd gone to college, waiting tables to pay for classes. She hadn't wanted a dime of her parents' money. She'd gotten a degree in helping other people. It didn't take much of a psychologist to figure out that Liam's words had influenced her career choice.

She'd survived. Found an inner strength she hadn't known existed. Left selfish and spoiled behind her.

Liam had walked away and never looked back.

"I hope you've been happy, Liam," she whispered from the window. "I never wished you ill."

She wasn't sure the same was true in what he wished for her.

Chapter Seven

She'd come after him?

A week later. But still… If he had known she had come looking for him, would it have made a difference? It was too late to ever know the answer to that now. Nearly a decade stood between them.

Vanessa looked so tiny standing over there by the window. He wanted to go and wrap his arms around her.

Not for the young woman he'd known then, but the woman she'd turned into now. Caring, passionate, using her strength for things that mattered.

No, he hadn't wished her any ill over the years. He'd been mad. Had sometimes thought about the few choice words he'd say to her if they ever happened to run into each other. But he'd never wished anything bad would happen to her.

He still felt as though he was missing part of the story. Something had happened between her and her parents, but evidently she didn't want to talk about it.

And maybe he should just leave it alone. He'd come here to lay the ghost of his past to rest. The hows and whys and should'ves and could'ves couldn't be changed and didn't matter.

But that kiss earlier. *That* he couldn't get out of his mind. His body started to respond just thinking about it. It was time to change the subject, move it away from the past and back to solving the case and saving those girls.

"I never wished you ill, either, Vanessa. Not ever."

She turned a little from the window and smiled slightly, nodding.

"How about if I don't ask any more questions and we concentrate on finding the other girls?"

She walked toward him. "Yes, I think that's a good idea."

"I need to contact Omega," he told her. "Unless you have someone else in mind, someone you know can be trusted, we should probably bring an outside doctor in to talk to Karine."

She nodded. "That's probably better. I do have lots of contacts at the hospital. I'm there quite a bit with my work. But all of them would probably believe the police over something a teenager says."

"Okay. I'll get rolling on that. Omega has contacts all over the country, not just in Colorado

Springs where headquarters is located. They should have someone here in a few hours."

"Good."

"Also, tell me where you found Karine. I can look at tide patterns, which will give us at least a general direction and possible distance she came from. We need to ask her how long she thinks she was swimming."

He walked over to a long drawer attached to a buffet in the dining room and pulled out large tidal maps of the area. Almost everyone who lived here year-round had a set. They were needed for just about any fishing or watersport activity.

He rolled out the one for their area. "Where did you find Karine?"

Vanessa stared at the map for longer than Liam expected. Was she confused? She'd always been so good with maps.

"We're here," he said, pointing to a spot on the map where his grandmother's house would be, not far from the Sound.

Then he noticed the blush that had stolen over her entire face.

"What?" he asked.

"Nothing." But her face was burning. "I was here when I found Karine." She pointed to a place on the map.

Oh.

Liam knew exactly where that was. Undoubtedly, by her flush, Vanessa knew exactly where that was, too.

A very secluded section of the Roanoke Sound where rarely anyone went. Its difficulty to access and mediocre views and beach made it not worth the effort by most. Sand dunes blocked it from the rest of the Sound.

It was their special place. The place where they'd gone when they'd wanted to get away from everything and everyone else.

They had made love there dozens of times. He could still remember the feel of the sun, of the sand, of the sweetness of Vanessa's body as if it had happened five minutes ago.

It was where Liam had asked her to marry him.

He didn't question why she'd been walking there yesterday and she didn't offer the information. Whatever reason she had been, he was glad; otherwise Karine might've been in a lot more trouble right now.

"Okay." He nodded. "You found her here at about 6:30 p.m., right?" He looked over at her for confirmation.

"Yes. Maybe a little closer to seven, but not much."

"We need to ask Karine how long she was swimming."

A soft voice answered from the doorway, "It felt like very long time."

Vanessa rushed over to the girl. "Hey, honey, how are you doing? Done sleeping?"

Karine looked down, embarrassed. "I am hungry again."

"That's fine. Let's get you some more food." She put her arm around the girl and led her to the kitchen. Liam followed them.

"How long do you think you swam, Karine? Do you have any idea how much time?" he asked as Vanessa began to make them all a sandwich.

"I do not know exact time," Karine said softly. "I swam until I could not move my arms anymore. Then I just used my legs. I was very cold."

Hours, then. But then again, Karine was not very big and hadn't had decent calorie intake in days or maybe weeks. So she might have become exhausted after just a few minutes.

Karine sat at the table and pulled her legs up to her chest, wrapping her arms around them. She was wearing the Outer Banks sweatshirt and sweatpants he'd bought at the grocery store. She rested her head on her knees and looked out across the room.

"We all were in same room that was in bottom of ship. Every morning and every evening, one of the three mans come. They bring food and water. Let us use bathroom and walk around. Sometimes choose a girl and drag her out." She wrapped her arms more tightly around her knees. "He said they would enjoy us for the week we were there."

Liam caught sight of Vanessa behind Karine. She had stopped what she was doing, listening, tears rolling down her cheeks. He didn't blame her. Anger burned like acid in his gut for what Karine had gone through, what the others were still going through.

"Karine, how many days had you been on the boat? Do you know?"

"That boat? *Divi*." She held up two fingers. "Two days. Before that, we were on other big ship for many, many days."

Karine's only having been on the little boat here in the Roanoke Sound for two days was good news. If the men planned to keep them for a week before selling the girls to whatever buyers they had lined up, that meant they still had five more days before the girls were forever out of their reach.

Unless the men decided to cut their losses and just kill the girls outright since Karine escaped. Liam prayed they would be too greedy to do that. Especially until they knew for sure someone was on to them.

"When man left yesterday morning, he did not close my…" She put her finger and thumb around her wrists in demonstration. "How you say?"

"Handcuff," Vanessa and Liam said in unison.

"Yes. He did not close my handcuff. I waited until he was gone, then showed the other girls. They agreed I should try to get help. They gave me all the day's food to eat." Now Karine began to cry. "I broke the door and got out."

"Could you see the land from the boat?" Since the boat was in the Sound, she could've been anywhere from half a mile—Liam didn't think the perps would dare keep a boat with kidnapped girls closer than half a mile in—to about four miles at the widest part of the Sound if the boat was being kept in the very center.

Honestly, Liam didn't think Karine would've made it that far. She would've drowned.

"Yes." Karine nodded. "I could see some land far away and some land closer. I swam toward the close one."

"Of course you did." Vanessa put a sandwich on the table in front of her. "Smart."

"Where was the sun when you got in the water? Straight overhead? Were you swimming toward it?"

Karine took a bite of her sandwich and thought as she chewed. "At first sun was straight, but then behind me." She shrugged.

"Good, that's good," Liam said. That meant she had been swimming east in the mid to late afternoon.

"Once I was on land I was too tired to walk. I slept for long time before I got up. Walked little more then lay down again. Miss Vanessa find me."

She would've been swimming with the tide, thank God. That undoubtedly was a factor in

Karine's making it to shore. Based on his knowledge of the area and the map, Liam could make an educated guess that the boat was in a certain two-mile radius on the Roanoke Sound. He took a pencil, wrote an X where Vanessa had found Karine and a circle where he thought it most likely the boat had been moored.

Unfortunately, there would probably be hundreds of boats in that same two-mile radius. Not to mention, the perps had probably already moved the boat. That was the main reason boats were so often used for human trafficking. Because they could be easily moved.

Vanessa put a plate with a sandwich next to him on the table. She looked over his shoulder at the map nodding.

"Now what do we do?" she asked.

"Now I make that call I was talking about earlier, getting the professional help needed."

"Good." Vanessa nodded, touching Karine gently on the shoulder. "That shouldn't wait."

"Then, if you think it's okay—" he turned to Karine to include her in the conversation, too "—and if it's all right with you, Karine, I think we should take a boat out to this area on the map—" he pointed with his finger "—to see if we can find anything."

"Do you think it's likely?" Vanessa asked.

"Honestly, no. But I do know that the longer we wait, the more endangered those girls become.

They are bound to move the boat soon if they haven't already."

"Yes." Karine was already standing. "Yes, Miss Vanessa. Please, let's look. We must try."

Liam could see Vanessa was torn. It was dangerous, he knew. Any number of people would be looking for both her and Karine.

"Is it worth the risk?" Vanessa asked softly. "I just can't stand the thought of anything happening to Karine."

Honestly, it probably wasn't worth the risk. The chances of them finding the girls were slim. But they were better than their chances of finding them from here in the house.

"I'm not going to let anything happen to you two. You can bet on that."

Chapter Eight

The search for the girls all that afternoon and the next day proved fruitless. Liam had rented a boat and taken them all around the area they'd determined on the map as the most likely place Karine had been held. But they hadn't found anything useful. Most likely the boat had already been moved. Vanessa's frustration mounted.

Liam was infinitely patient when working with Karine. He showed her different boat sizes so she could have a reference to better describe the one she'd been held in. He pointed out landmarks she might have seen in the distance while swimming that might have been familiar. He never got frustrated with her no matter what she could or couldn't remember.

Even though his focus had been torn—looking for boats that could be holding the kidnapped girls and also for anyone who might be trying to find Vanessa and Karine—he was never short with

Karine when she asked any questions or had any sort of language barrier that needed clarification. It was easy to see that Karine was becoming more comfortable with Liam.

Liam would make a great father.

Maybe he was already a father. The thought cut something deep inside Vanessa. Eight years was a long time. He could've been married before. Have a whole gaggle of kids.

"What? Are you okay?" Liam was looking at her. Reaching out one arm from where he was steering the boat. "Are you sick?"

"Have you ever been married? Do you have any kids?" The questions were out of her mouth before she could stop them.

He tilted his head to the side. "How do you know I'm not married now?"

"You never would've kissed me at the hotel if you were." Vanessa had never even questioned that. Liam would be true to the woman he married.

"No, never married. No kids." He grinned in that way that was so uniquely Liam and winked at her. "Although many of my colleagues would argue that *I* am a kid."

She couldn't help smiling back. "I don't doubt it."

He nodded and then turned his face back to watch the water in front of them, answering a question Karine had.

Although the search hadn't led to any positive results, the doctor Omega Sector had sent, Dr. Jennifer Giandomenico, both a medical doctor and psychiatrist, had been wonderful. She had been waiting when they'd returned from searching the Sound yesterday afternoon. She had examined Karine and documented all possible physical evidence in case it was needed later. Then she had talked with the girl for hours.

Vanessa wasn't sure exactly what the doctor had said to the girl, or what Karine had said to the doctor, but Karine had looked better, calmer, after their conversation.

Omega Sector had also sent profiler Andrea Gordon to help out in any way she was needed: profiling, surveillance, hanging out with Karine.

Vanessa had wanted to dislike the agent—the young, gorgeous, leggy blonde agent—on sight. Was this the type of colleague Liam worked with all the time at Omega?

But the woman had been nothing short of immaculately professional with both her and Liam. No flirting, no touches with him or anything that could be considered unprofessional. As a matter of fact, Vanessa would have thought Andrea was downright cold if it wasn't for how she treated Karine. Andrea might be all business with her and Liam, but with Karine she was friendly and kind. Something in Andrea identified with Karine, Vanessa could see.

Vanessa had to go back to work today. She had called in sick the past two days, but any more than that would really be suspicious. She'd be wearing the same jeans and blouse she'd worn three days ago—she'd washed them yesterday—since she didn't dare stop by her house to get new clothes. Fortunately the organization she worked for—a privately funded aid organization that helped families, women and children in need—encouraged casual dress. Many of the people Vanessa went out to see and help on a daily basis would not respond well to a suit.

"Remember, be as vague as possible when answering any questions your colleagues ask," Liam told her. "Cough a lot and tell them you're still not feeling one hundred percent. That will usually keep people away."

Liam was going to drop her about three blocks from the hotel where they'd left her car. She was going to drive to work from there.

"The police are still looking for their 'fugitive,' so don't freak out if you're pulled over," Liam told her. "Just let them search your car then move on. Don't ask questions."

"How long do you think they'll keep doing that?"

Liam shrugged. "It's a smart move on the perp's part, actually. Having a fugitive on the loose provides them with an opportunity to search cars—

in the name of citizen safety—they'd otherwise need a warrant to search."

"I know a few cops. Why don't I use my contacts at work to see if I can find out who provided the information about said fugitive? That would give us our bad guy, right?"

Liam shrugged. "Maybe. Or maybe it would just be someone who was following someone else's orders." He helped her slip on her button-down sweater. "Don't do anything that will draw attention to yourself or the trafficking ring. Our greatest asset right now is making them think that Karine made it to shore, you helped her and she ran without telling anyone anything. If they think we know about them, it might make them move up their timetable or do something drastic."

"Okay." Vanessa nodded. *Drastic* meant kill the girls. That was the last thing she wanted.

"Andrea is going to rent a house on the other side of the island in her name. If somebody recognizes me, this place won't be usable as a safe house any longer. Our past history is too well known."

She looked over to where Andrea and Karine were eating cereal and watching old sitcom reruns on television.

"Yeah, Karine seems pretty comfortable with her. I think that will be good." She watched as the two females looked at each other then laughed at something on the television. "How old is Andrea, anyway?"

Liam cocked his head to the side. "I'm not sure. I never thought about it. She pretty much keeps to herself all the time at work. I guess I assumed she was in her late twenties."

Vanessa doubted the woman was over twenty-two or twenty-three, although she didn't voice her opinion. Andrea tried hard—maybe a little too hard in Vanessa's opinion—to be professional. But underneath, Andrea seemed to be much more relaxed and carefree. Maybe she just felt she needed to keep up a front around her coworkers. Vanessa didn't care, because the woman seemed as drawn to Karine as Karine was to her. Kindred spirits.

"Okay, I'm ready," she said to Liam. "'Bye, girls," she called out to Andrea and Karine. They both waved but barely even looked at her. Vanessa rolled her eyes. At least she didn't have to worry about Karine being upset she was leaving.

Liam opened the door for her at his SUV. "After work, drive straight back to your house. Try to act as normal as possible. Text me and we'll work out a plan. Andrea is going to get Karine a phone today, too, so she can talk to you or text if she needs something."

That was good. Vanessa knew both Liam and Andrea were competent and cared about what happened to Karine. But Vanessa felt responsible for her. She wanted the girl to be able to easily get in touch with her if she needed something.

"Great. Thank you." Vanessa was nervous. Jittery.

When they were almost to where Liam was going to drop her off, he reached over and grabbed her hand. It was lying on the leg she couldn't quite keep from bouncing with nervous energy.

He looked over at her. "You're going to do fine. It's just another day at the office."

"I'm not a great liar. I've always just voiced my opinions about everything, usually not caring what other people thought." She shrugged and looked away. She was certain that was part of why he thought her so selfish and self-centered.

He squeezed her hand. "Honesty is a trait to be admired, so don't beat yourself up over it. Just don't volunteer information and try to sidestep any questions."

Easier said than done.

He stopped at the parking lot of a diner a few blocks from the hotel where her car was parked. He turned off the SUV and looked at her. "The key to a good lie is to keep it as close to the truth as you can. If anyone seems suspicious about how you're behaving, take them into your confidence."

She shot him a blank look, frowning.

He turned toward her and leaned a little closer. "Tell them, in truth, you weren't really sick but called in because your old flame showed up in town and the two of you were naked in a hotel room before you even knew what happened."

VANESSA WAS STILL thinking about Liam's outrageous statement two hours later when she sat at her desk pretending she was catching up on paperwork. Not only the statement but the kiss that had come afterward.

She was sure he'd probably meant it as a playful, go-get-'em, tiger-type kiss. Instead, within seconds they'd been all but crawling over each other. Continued proof there were some things time didn't change. The heat between the two of them was one of those things.

When they had finally broken apart, Vanessa had been halfway over the center console into his lap and both of them were breathing heavily. The windows were completely steamed up and Vanessa's blouse was half unbuttoned.

It had taken them five minutes before they could pull it together enough to even get out a coherent sentence. By then Vanessa had no idea what she would say to him, so she had straightened her shirt and bailed out the door, walking to her car without looking back at Liam.

But she'd felt his eyes on her. And known what his look meant. And everything in her body had tightened at the thought as she walked.

So yeah, making up something about how her old flame was in town and had gotten her completely discombobulated would not be any stretch of the truth at all.

Fortunately, nobody seemed to care. Everyone was busy with their own set of issues—there was always more than enough work to go around—and didn't even notice if Vanessa looked a little flush. Or if they did they just attributed it to whatever supposed sickness she'd had for the past two days.

Vanessa had multiple voice-mail messages on her phone. Some were from families she worked with, which she listened to and took notes on. Two were from Judy in the hospital.

"Hey, Vanessa, it's Judy. I just checked you and that teenage girl in a few minutes ago. Then the police showed up looking for her and you guys were gone. I just want to make sure you're okay. She didn't look like much of a threat, but you just never know with some of these kids today. Call me."

Another one from her the next day.

"Hi, Vanessa, it's Judy again. I talked to your boss and she said you'd called in sick. I just wanted to make sure you were really okay. The police came by here again this afternoon looking for you or that girl. Just want to talk to you for myself to make sure you're okay. Call me."

She'd better call her friend before Judy did something crazy such as go to the police herself with concerns about Vanessa's behavior. Vanessa liked Judy a lot, but the older woman did tend to be a bit paranoid.

Vanessa was just picking up her phone when it buzzed on her desk. She pressed the intercom button to talk to her boss.

"What's up, Maureen?"

"Vanessa, can you come out to the lobby? There are two officers here and they said you need to go with them to the sheriff's office for questioning."

Chapter Nine

Vanessa hung up with Maureen and immediately called Liam. He picked up on the first ring.

"What's wrong?"

"The police are here." She tried to keep the panic out of her voice but couldn't quite manage. "What do I do?"

"Damn it," Liam muttered. "They must have been watching your office. We knew this was a possibility. Just stick with the story of me and you as lovers. That will also be corroborated by Officer Atwood's statement from what he saw on Tuesday."

"Okay," she whispered, staying hidden behind her door so no one could see her from the clear windows opening out to the lobby. "But I thought we were trying not to let them know who you are."

"I'm sure it will be suspicious that an Omega agent just happened to show up the day after one of the victims escaped."

She could hear the tension in Liam's voice.

"But the perp might buy that you and I are just rekindling our relationship."

She gripped the cell tighter. "But he might not. Which would put the girls in danger."

The phone on her desk buzzed again.

"I've got to go," she whispered.

"See if you can keep my name out of it, but if you need to tell them it's me, that's okay, Nessa. All right?"

There was a loud knock on her office door. Evidently the officers were tired of waiting.

"I'll do my best. Bye."

She disconnected the call and slipped the phone into her purse. She didn't know if she'd be allowed to use it again or not once they took her to the station.

She opened the door. "Can I help you, gentlemen?"

"Vanessa Epperson, we need you to come with us to the sheriff's office."

"Guys, I've been out sick for two days." She glanced over their shoulders and saw that everyone in her entire office was watching the spectacle. "I've got a ton of paperwork and cases that need my attention. Does this need to be done right this second? Could you come back tomorrow?"

"No, ma'am," one of the officers, the shorter, chunkier one, said. "We've been instructed to bring you in right now."

"Am I under arrest? Are you going to put me in handcuffs?" Vanessa laughed lightly, but neither man even cracked a smile.

"Only if you refuse to come with us, ma'am."

"Fine." Vanessa walked over and made a show of straightening papers and organizing her desk. She knew she was stalling but didn't know why. There was no help coming.

She didn't want to be arrested. Didn't want to answer their questions. Didn't want to take a chance on letting Liam and Karine down by saying something wrong.

When the officers stepped closer to her, she gave up. She just put everything down and went with them. She didn't want to be arrested in front of her colleagues, but they were all staring at her as if she were already in handcuffs anyway, so she guessed it didn't matter.

"I'll be back later, Maureen," she said as she passed her boss, both officers flanking her. "Sorry for the ruckus."

As the men put her in the back of their police car, Vanessa vaguely wondered if anyone else would think it was overkill that the department had sent two large officers to bring her—half their size and weight—in. Probably not.

The drive was short to the sheriff's office. Vanessa expected to be fingerprinted or have her mug shot taken or something. She realized she really didn't have a good idea of what happened on this side of law enforcement.

Liam would. He'd been here often enough when he was younger, and he worked in law enforcement now. But Vanessa was determined not to bring up his name no matter what.

They brought her into an interrogation room—she'd seen enough television shows and movies to recognize the two-way mirror for what it was—sat her at a table that had four uncomfortable chairs, read her the Miranda rights and left.

Nobody came in and yelled at her. Nobody came in and threatened her with jail time. Nobody took her belongings or searched her person. As a matter of fact, they were nice enough to leave a bottle of water out on the table. So Vanessa waited.

And waited.

She had a signal on her cell phone, but she didn't want to make any calls or send any texts. She was sure this room was being watched, to see what she did, who she contacted.

Finally, more than an hour after she'd been placed in the room, someone came in. Handsome, young, maybe not even as old as Vanessa's twenty-eight years. But it was plain to see he was all-business, looking to make a name for himself.

She disliked him on sight.

"I'm Assistant Sheriff Tommy Webb," he said,

sitting across from her at the table. "You've been read your rights, correct, Miss Epperson?"

"Do I need a lawyer?" she asked.

The man cocked his head sideways and gave her a smile she was sure was meant to put her at ease.

Liam would've done it much better.

"I've found that criminals are the only ones who need lawyers, Miss Epperson. But, certainly, it is your right, if you'd like to call one."

It was probably better to try to get out of this without a lawyer. Not that she knew one to call, anyway. Her parents had one on retainer, but Vanessa wouldn't call him even if she knew the contact info.

"I don't need a lawyer."

"Good." Webb looked pleased with himself. "Let's just start with an easy question, like, where have you been for the past couple of days?"

That wasn't an easy question at all. It was probably one of the most difficult questions he could ask. Vanessa thought fast. Should she try to pretend she'd been sick? Or should she do as Liam had suggested and bring him into the equation?

Of course, she also wanted to keep his identity a secret so they didn't know an Omega Sector agent was sniffing around their backyard.

"You called in sick to work, Miss Epperson," Assistant Sheriff Webb said, probably trying to make her think they knew quite a bit about it. But she knew they didn't know the truth. "Why don't you start there?"

She would follow Liam's advice and go with the "hot lovers" story. That was pretty darn close to the truth anyway.

"Look, Officer Webb..."

"Assistant Sheriff Webb," he corrected.

Vanessa barely refrained from rolling her eyes. "Assistant Sheriff Webb." She leaned a little closer in her chair. "Is what we say here going to be reported back to my boss?"

"We're under no obligation to report what you say here to your boss."

Vanessa noticed he didn't actually say they *wouldn't* tell her boss, but she left it alone. "Okay, yeah, I called in sick, but I wasn't actually sick."

"You were with someone," Webb continued for her.

"I'm sure you don't want all the dirty little details, but it was a guy that I met last year and he came back into town. Things got pretty hot and heavy between us."

"Can you provide us with his name?"

Damn it. "Um, no."

Assistant Sheriff Webb's eyebrow rose. "Why not?"

"Let's just say he, um, wasn't supposed to be with me. And that he has a definite aversion to anything having to do with the police."

Webb wrote down a bunch of notes. Probably

that Liam was a criminal or married or something. Good. The more shady they thought him, the better.

"We'll come back to that," he said. "You were with him for the whole two days?"

"Yep." Vanessa smiled dreamily, which wasn't too difficult when she thought about her kiss with Liam this morning. "That Officer Atwood guy who came to the hotel Tuesday morning saw us."

"Yes, but that was early Tuesday. Did you stay at that hotel until this morning?" Webb didn't look up from his notes as he asked the question.

Because they knew she hadn't been there. Webb was hoping to catch her in a lie.

"No." Vanessa shook her head. "We went to another place. I think the cop kind of freaked my friend out."

"And where was that place?"

Vanessa realized she was digging herself in deeper. "I don't mean to be rude, but what is this all about? I haven't done anything wrong... Well, at least not illegal, and neither has my *friend*. Why do you have so many questions about what I've been doing the past couple of days?"

Webb didn't respond, obviously trying to decide whether to push it or not.

It was time to take a page out of the Liam Goetz playbook: stand naked in the doorway.

"Look, I'll be glad to give you a blow-by-blow," she snickered a little at that, "of the entire past forty-eight hours. What we did at a friend of a friend's house. On the bed. And on the kitchen table. And even right outside on the back deck. Come to think of it, maybe we did do something illegal. But I don't think that's what you want to write down in your little notebook."

She leaned back in her seat and crossed her arms over her chest, feigning a smug confidence she didn't have.

Liam would be proud if he could see her right now. She knew it without a doubt.

And it worked. Webb grimaced and took some papers out of another file on the table. "Fine, if your actions for the past couple days are not fit to be written, then let's talk about the girl you picked up on Monday evening."

Vanessa rolled her eyes as if she was bored. "Seriously? I told that officer guy all I knew about her."

"And what was that?"

It was important for her to remember the details she'd told Officer Atwood. "She was walking on the side of the road. I'm in social work, like you know, so I was concerned about her. I took her to 7-Eleven for some food and Gatorade."

"Did you talk to her? Ask her about her situation?"

"She didn't say much. Honestly, I think she was probably on something. She didn't really seem to understand much of what I said."

Hopefully, if Webb was the one in on the trafficking ring, he would think Vanessa just thought Karine had been on drugs, not that she'd noticed the girl was from a different country.

"So what did you do after getting her something to eat and drink?"

"I took her to the hospital. She still seemed dehydrated and possibly on drugs. More help than I could give her. Plus, I had other plans for the night."

"So you didn't really talk to her and you didn't really care what happened to her. You just dumped her at the hospital. Odd behavior for a social worker."

"It wasn't like that. Look, most of the time I get up early and work late to help people. Any of the families I partner with can attest to that. But I had plans, so I couldn't take this kid on."

"It sort of looks like you took the kid on." He took a picture and slid it over to Vanessa. It was of security footage of her and Karine at the hospital, Vanessa hovering close and protectively over the girl.

Vanessa shrugged. "I'm not a monster. Just because I couldn't stay there with her doesn't mean I didn't care about what happened to her."

"We need to find this girl, Miss Epperson." Webb's voice took on a very grim tone.

Vanessa watched as his face seemed to get harder, eyes flintier.

Yeah, this guy was pretty desperate to get his hands on Karine.

Too desperate.

Webb took out some other pictures and placed them in front of Vanessa. "These are from Tuesday night, the night after you dropped the teenager at the hospital."

The pictures weren't very clear, no real visual of a face, but it was definitely someone with long brown hair, about Karine's height and build. The person was obviously robbing a house, grabbing valuables and stuffing them in a bag.

"Is that her?" Vanessa asked. She knew very well it wasn't Karine, but played along. "Officer Atwood mentioned something about her being wanted for burglary."

Webb slid the pictures back and then took out another stack. "Unfortunately, your teenage runaway is now wanted for more than burglary. When the woman whose house she broke into came home, she hit her in the head with a metal fire poker. The woman died."

Vanessa gasped as the next set of pictures Webb set out showed the girl hitting a woman and the woman falling to the ground.

"Evidently the suspect didn't realize there was a security camera at the house." He pulled out another picture. "Moreover, the person she was with didn't realize there was a camera, either."

He pushed another picture in front of her. A

woman, also dressed in black, like the one who had brandished the fire poker, stood by the shadow in the doors.

Again, you couldn't make out many details about the person. But her height, her build, the hair coming out from under the dark ball cap she wore?

Looked quite similar to Vanessa.

"This was Tuesday night?" she finally blurted. The pictures were jarring. The knowledge that someone seemed to be setting her up even more so.

"That person." He pointed to the woman in the shadow. "Looks pretty similar to you."

"That's n-not me," Vanessa stuttered.

Assistant Sheriff Webb's eyes were hard. "I'm getting a lot of pressure to get this case solved, Miss Epperson. More than that, I'm *determined* to catch the person who did this—whether it's your teenager friend or not—and the woman she was with."

Vanessa swallowed. "That's not me. And I don't know the location of the girl you're looking for. I can't help you. I'm sorry."

"Well, you are our best link in this case. Our only link right now. So you have two choices— you either provide me with the name of the man you were supposedly with for the past forty-eight hours for an alibi, or we arrest you and continue this questioning later."

Chapter Ten

As soon as Vanessa had disconnected the call with Liam, he sprang into action.

"Ladies." He didn't want to frighten Karine, so he kept his tone as light as possible. "I don't mean to interrupt your television viewing, but we need to vacate a little sooner than planned."

Andrea was on her feet in an instant.

"Trouble?" she said softly.

"Locals picked up Vanessa."

Andrea grimaced. "I'll get dressed."

"What means *vacate*?" Karine asked as she brought the cereal bowls over and began washing them in the sink.

"It means leave. We knew we needed to go to another house, remember? We're just having to do it a little earlier than we'd planned." He touched her shoulder gently, slowly. It was the first time he'd initiated any sort of physical contact, and was glad when the girl didn't flinch or pull away.

"Miss Vanessa?" Karine asked.

"She'll be fine. Promise." He'd see to it personally. "She'll meet us there soon, okay?"

"Okay." She reached up and squeezed his hand.

They were completely packed and ready to leave less than twenty minutes later. He and Karine followed Andrea as she went to a local rental property office and secured a house for the next two weeks. Then they drove to the house.

Andrea had chosen well. It was a great location, directly on the Roanoke Sound, but far enough away from the action that no one would accidentally stumble onto them. It had a boat dock and a small fishing boat, which could allow for a second means of escape if needed.

Most of all, the rental agreement was solely in Andrea's name. There was no tie whatsoever to Vanessa or Liam. So if something happened to them—although Liam planned to make sure that didn't happen—Karine would still be safe. Andrea would get her out. Hell, the only reason they didn't get her out right now was to help the other girls. But if they had to, Omega could have a helicopter in here and out again in under an hour. The sheriff's department would be none the wiser.

But that was a last resort and only if there was no hope for getting the other girls out alive. Karine would not leave them behind willingly.

Once Andrea and Karine were safely in the house, Liam left. He had to get to the sheriff's office to see about Vanessa. Hopefully she was holding up under the questioning. They wouldn't have any grounds to hold her, he was sure—you couldn't be arrested for helping a runaway teenager—but knew that questioning could be uncomfortable at best. Downright wearying at worst.

Everything in him said to get her out of there right now. Liam was a man of action. But he knew in this case, rushing in there, pulling rank—and he could do it—wouldn't help their cause. Wouldn't help those girls.

Vanessa was strong. She could handle it.

He put a call in to his boss at Omega on his way to the sheriff's office. If things went sour, he was going to need backup. More than just Andrea could provide.

"Liam. How's it going?" Steve Drackett asked as soon as the call was connected.

"Locals have taken Vanessa in for questioning." Steve already knew about the trafficking ring from when Liam had called and Andrea had been sent.

"Okay, let me put someone on that to get info. Hang on."

Steve was back on the line in just a few moments. "What's your plan?"

"I'm on my way to the station now. So far my presence on the island, and the fact that I'm law enforcement, is unknown. Vanessa is trying to keep me unknown to them, but I'm not sure if she'll hold up."

"That's a lot for someone with no training to keep hidden during questioning. You. Karine. The trafficking ring."

"Exactly." Liam took a turn. He was almost there. That was the good thing about the Outer Banks islands being so small—nothing was too far away. "Andrea has already gotten Karine to a new safe house, so even if Vanessa crumbles, they won't find her anywhere having to do with me."

"Good. What do you need?"

"If we can keep whoever is behind this thinking we don't know anything about the trafficking ring, I think we have four more days until the sale goes down. Bastards wanted to use the girls themselves for a little while."

Liam heard Steve's curse and agreed with the word he'd said. "I'm going to go ahead and send Derek and Joe. You'll need them."

When they found out exactly where the girls were being held and it came down to actually getting them out, there was no one Liam would want more at his back than Derek Waterman and Joe Matarazzo. They'd saved his ass more than once.

"It will probably be a couple days at the most." Liam pulled into a parking spot at the sheriff's office.

Steve cursed again.

"What?"

"It looks like someone is trying to run a warrant through to arrest your girl."

"*What?* For what?" Liam's teeth ground.

"Aiding and abetting a criminal."

"Damn it. It looks like I might need to blow my cover here, Steve. I'm not going to let them arrest her if I can be her alibi."

"I agree. But be careful."

"I'll call with an update later." Liam disconnected the call and was jogging across the parking lot in moments. As he got to the stairs he was stopped by someone sitting on a bench under a tree right outside the door.

"Liam Goetz. I should've known if Vanessa was about to be arrested, you would be somewhere in close vicinity."

George Epperson. Vanessa's father.

Liam stopped. "What are you doing here? Did Vanessa call you?" Liam shouldn't be surprised at that. Vanessa had always been able to call her parents whenever she wanted something—a trip to Paris, a diamond bracelet—and they'd made it happen. This situation wouldn't be any different.

The man's soft bark of laughter held no humor whatsoever. "No, my daughter very definitely did not call me. Fortunately, I have friends here at the station. Or rather, I should say, people who want to stay in my good graces. One of them let me know she was here."

"Oh." The man looked older, much older, than

he had when Liam had last seen him. Eight years ago when Liam had gone to his house, asking to see Vanessa, wanting to know why she hadn't showed up at their planned location to meet and go get married.

George Epperson had made it very clear that his daughter was no longer interested in marrying a "hoodlum—reformed or not" and that Liam was not ever welcome on their property again.

Obviously, Epperson's attitude toward Liam hadn't changed very much. But he couldn't get over how much more haggard the man looked. Maybe he had health problems or something.

"My lawyer is inside with her right now, taking care of whatever charges the department is threatening to bring together."

Relief flowed through Liam. He might not be a personal fan of George Epperson's, but if his money and lawyer got Vanessa out of the sheriff's office unscathed, Liam would be the first to applaud. Not to mention that Epperson had just saved Liam from going in there and pulling out his badge—putting those kidnapped girls in extreme danger. So if Epperson wanted to blame him for Vanessa being in this mess, it was a small price to pay.

"Did you do something to her? With her?" Epperson asked. "I understand the possible charge against her is aiding and abetting a criminal. That sounds about up your alley."

Either Epperson didn't remember that Liam had been entering the DEA when they'd last met or he just didn't care. The man had never been able to get much past Liam's run-ins with the law when he'd been a teenager. As far as George had been concerned, Liam had never been good enough for his daughter.

Liam didn't know what the man had to be so bitter about now. In the unspoken war between them—Liam had never thought of it that way, but figured Epperson had—the older man had definitely won.

For years when he was younger, Liam had held his tongue around Mr. Epperson. Vanessa loved her family and Liam hadn't wanted to force a wedge between them. But he and Vanessa had both known her parents were never going to give them their blessing for a wedding, so they had agreed to get married and then just tell them. At least that was what Liam had thought they'd agreed. Until Vanessa hadn't showed up.

Liam took a step closer to the man so he wouldn't have to speak louder. "You know I'm law enforcement. Knew it when I left. I'm here to help Vanessa, not get her in any trouble."

Epperson shrugged, not willing to admit it. The look he gave Liam made him feel as if he were still twenty years old and bringing her home from a date. He'd always respected the Eppersons' rules and had always had her home on time, but it had never been enough. Epperson had always looked at Liam just as he was looking at Liam now: like an annoyance and a peasant.

Liam shook his head. Some things never changed. "I don't know why you still hate me. You never thought I was good enough for Vanessa. I get that. And, honestly, Mr. Epperson, I even understand it. But why in God's name would you still dislike me so much now?"

Liam knew he should stop, that he should just walk away, but couldn't bring himself to do it. "She didn't marry me. Obviously she agreed with you about me not being good enough. She chose you guys. You've still got her."

The look on Epperson's face changed. All the years came crushing down on his countenance and he looked so old to Liam, although he couldn't have been more than his mid-fifties.

"You're an idiot, Goetz." There was no sting to the words. "We're both idiots."

Liam cocked his head to the side. That second comment he hadn't expected. "Not that I disagree, but what are you talking about?"

For the first time George looked at Liam like a person, an equal. "Liam, I'm pretty sure you don't know all the facts about—"

"What are you doing here?"

Liam's words were cut off by Vanessa's hiss behind him. At first he thought she meant him, coming here and possibly ruining his cover. But when he turned he found all her anger focused on her father.

Epperson shrugged. "I got word that you were being detained. So I called Michaels and had him meet me here."

The emotional distance between Vanessa and her father was palpable. When Liam had known Vanessa before, she hadn't always agreed with her parents, had thought they were old-fashioned and overprotective, but they had always been close. She'd always been the apple of her father's eye.

Now it looked as though she wasn't interested in being her father's anything. She wasn't even interested in being in his presence.

"You shouldn't have come here at all, Dad. Shouldn't have sent Michaels."

"It's good your father sent his lawyer, Vanessa," Liam told her. "I didn't have to break my cover. I was on my way to do just that."

She took a deep breath. "Yes, you're right," she said to Liam. Then she turned to her father. "I do appreciate your help. There's a situation—I'm not at liberty to talk about it—but your assistance really helped. So, thank you. But, Dad, I still want you to stay out of my life."

"Vanessa…" Mr. Epperson said, reaching his hand toward her.

She stepped away from him. "Save it, Dad. As always, too little, too late."

Liam didn't really understand what was happening between Vanessa and George. Obviously this chasm between them wasn't anything new; both knew where they stood in this battle and were accustomed to the war.

Liam would've thought seeing an emotional distance between Vanessa and her family would make him happy. Would make him feel justified.

Instead it just left him with a lingering sadness.

It was another piece of the puzzle, an important piece, to understanding exactly what had happened between him and Vanessa, but Liam had no idea where the piece went.

Why would Vanessa tell her father to *continue* to stay out of her life? Something must have drastically changed in the past eight years. Was it long ago? More recent?

Whichever, Liam found himself wanting to help the two of them bridge whatever gap lay between them. While Epperson looked as if he would give anything to sit and talk with his daughter—hell, Liam even felt sorry for the man—Vanessa was obviously not interested.

She turned to Liam. "Are you ready? You sticking around out here is probably not the best idea."

She was right. He nodded.

Epperson sighed. "At least call your mother. She is worried about you. She's always worried about you—in your line of work—but now she's even more distraught."

Vanessa rolled her eyes. "Social work isn't dangerous, Dad."

It was obviously not a new conversation.

"I know. But your mother...worries."

"Fine. I'll call her in a few days." She turned to Liam. "Let's go." She didn't wait for him, just began walking.

Epperson looked at Vanessa as she stalked off. Then he turned to Liam. "Like I said, we're both idiots."

He turned and walked off without another word, joining his lawyer at the doorway to the station. Liam jogged in the direction of Vanessa in the parking lot.

"Whoa," he said when he reached her. "Are you okay?"

He saw her quickly reach up and wipe her eyes with the back of her hand.

"Vanessa—"

"No, I don't want to talk about it. I just want to get out of here."

He took her arm and led her in the direction of the SUV. "You don't want to talk about your father or you don't want to talk about the questioning?"

"My father."

"Okay." He helped her inside the vehicle then went around to the driver's side. When he got in, she had her head laid back against the seat rest, eyes closed. Her stomach growled loudly in the silence.

It was already midafternoon. She had to be starving. "Food first. Then we'll talk."

She nodded. "But don't go far. We'll need to come back here."

"Is that such a good idea?"

"I want us to follow someone."

"Who?"

"Assistant Sheriff Tommy Webb, the guy who was questioning me. I think he's the one who's behind the trafficking ring."

Chapter Eleven

They got fast-food burgers and immediately headed back to the sheriff's office parking lot. Vanessa explained everything that had happened in questioning.

"Obviously those pictures can't be Karine," Vanessa said between bites. "She was with us the entire time."

"Someone is setting up a case against her. A preemptive strike," Liam said. "So if she does come forward with her story, they'll be able to discredit her."

"Killing someone?" Vanessa shook her head. "I can't believe they'd go to that length."

Liam's real concern now was for those other girls. Someone willing to kill a complete stranger to possibly discredit Karine would not hesitate to kill the other girls to keep themselves from getting caught.

They were running out of time.

"It sounds like you did good in there," he said.

"I don't know. I tried." She shrugged. "That guy Webb is determined to catch Karine. Like 'nothing will get in my way' sort of determined."

Liam chuckled at her imitation of Webb. "Who is he? I don't recognize him from when I lived here."

"No, he's young to be assistant sheriff. Mid-twenties maybe? He's all about the power."

Liam had already called Omega for any info about Webb. That should be coming in soon.

It was a long shot, but a long shot was better than doing nothing.

Vanessa had been texting Karine pretty constantly since he'd given her the girl's new phone number. Karine was happy with Andrea. They were watching television again and about to eat dinner. Liam could tell that knowing Karine was safe took a lot of stress off Vanessa.

Now they were waiting for Webb to leave so they could follow him. It might be a while. They were sitting in a section of the parking lot where they had a good line of sight of the back door and the parking area the officers used. When Webb came out, they would see him.

Liam rolled down the windows a little bit to let some breeze through the SUV and then asked the question that had been on his mind for the past hour.

"What's going on between you and your parents, Vanessa?"

Her sigh was audible. "I don't want to talk about it."

"He saved our asses, you know, by bringing in his lawyer to get you out." Liam was a little irritated that he hadn't thought of the plan. It was perfect. Who would Vanessa call if she was in trouble?

Daddy.

No one would've suspected a thing. It would've kept him, and especially the fact that he was law enforcement, out of the equation.

"We should've made that the plan from the beginning," Liam continued. "You calling your father for help."

"I wouldn't have agreed to it."

She would've. To save those girls, Liam was convinced, Vanessa would do just about anything. But that wasn't the point he wanted to argue with her. What he wanted to know was why there was such a rift between her and her dad.

"Why?"

"We don't talk anymore."

"At all?" Liam could hardly believe that. She was the Eppersons' only child. They doted on her. Spoiled her. Gave her all their love and attention.

"No, not really. Although my mom calls, so I let her know I'm okay."

"Did you guys get in a fight? George said your

mom worries about you doing social work—is that it?" Liam could understand Mrs. Epperson's concern. But for it to cause a rift of this size between them?

"No, that's not really it."

"Then what?"

She stared at him in the gathering darkness from the sun's descent. For a long time he didn't think she was going to answer him.

"We fought. It was a long time ago. I don't really want to talk about it."

Liam couldn't seem to let it go. Even if he'd never been accepted by them, he knew how much Vanessa loved her parents. "You can't find a way to work it out? I know how close you all are… were."

"Some things just can't be fixed. The shattered pieces are too many to be glued back together."

That same look he recognized from the hotel Tuesday morning was back in her eyes: pain, loss, emptiness.

Liam found the resentment he'd held toward her for the past few years begin to melt away. Yeah, she'd hurt him, broken his heart when she'd changed her mind about marrying him. He'd nursed that wound for a lot of years.

But whatever had happened to her since he'd left—whatever had put that look in her eyes— Liam was willing to let go of all his past anger and hurt if it meant he'd never have to see that look on her face again. That heaviness, as if she carried the weight of the world on her small shoulders.

"Nessa—"

"I can't talk about it, Liam." She buried her face in her hands. "I'm sorry."

He reached over and smoothed his hand down her hair. "You don't have to talk about it, okay? I'm here. I just want you to know I'm here and you don't have to carry whatever this is alone anymore if you don't want to."

He could tell she was wiping tears from her eyes. Then she leaned her face into his hand, which had moved to cup her cheek.

The heat was there between them. It always had been and probably always would be. But there was something more between them now.

A warmth.

"I'm sorry you were so hurt eight years ago," she whispered.

"You were twenty. I was twenty-two. God forbid we be judged for the rest of our lives solely by the decisions we made at that age."

She nodded and started to say something else but then their attention was caught when the back door of the station opened. It was Webb.

"Showtime," Liam murmured.

The man didn't seem suspicious, not looking around for anyone tailing him, but that didn't necessarily mean anything. They followed him to a nearby diner, where he went inside and fortunately sat by a window booth. They could see that two other men joined him.

Three men. Just as Karine had mentioned.

What Liam wouldn't give for audio surveillance on them right now.

"Do you think that's them?" Vanessa whispered.

"I don't know, but it sure seems possible."

They watched for verbal cues as the men talked, but without knowing the topic, understanding their expressions and gestures was impossible.

Liam's phone buzzed and he looked down at it. It was the report about Tommy Webb. He read through it.

"What?" Vanessa asked when Liam grimaced.

"It's the background info Omega Sector sent me about Tommy Webb."

"Something bad?"

Liam shook his head. "The opposite, actually. The guy was literally a Boy Scout. Grew up in Raleigh but vacationed here. After he went to college—with a 4.0 GPA, by the way—he moved to the Outer Banks. Was a deputy and then worked his way up to assistant sheriff. Pretty impressive for someone twenty-six years old. He's driven."

"So he's not our guy?"

"Not necessarily. He could still be behind the trafficking ring. But if so, he's very good at making himself look like what he's not."

"Well, whoever made the video of 'Karine' hitting someone with a fire iron is also good at making stuff look like something it's not," Vanessa shot back, leaning forward to look closer at the men in the diner.

She was right. It looked as though Webb was a perfectionist. That could translate very well to running a successful human-trafficking ring.

Except for one small girl who'd bravely escaped. The cog in Webb's wheel.

They needed to know who those other guys were. Liam cursed again at their lack of surveillance equipment.

"I'm going to go in and try to get pictures of the two other men with my phone," he told Vanessa.

"What if someone recognizes you?"

"I'll have to take the chance. We have to know who those guys are and get someone following them." Liam was thankful Derek and Joe were on their way. They were needed.

Stress was clear on Vanessa's face. "Be careful."

He reached over and gave her a quick, forceful kiss.

"Hey." He winked at her. "It's me."

She was still rolling her eyes when Liam grabbed a ball cap from the backseat and hopped out the door. He pulled the cap low over his head and prayed no one would recognize him as he went inside.

He sat at the bar and immediately ordered coffee. The waitress smiled as she brought it, but Liam didn't engage in any casual conversation with her. That might just call the men's attention toward them.

Liam tried to make it so his phone would take a picture of the men from the back lens. That way it would appear that Liam was looking at his screen—as almost everyone in the diner was—but, really, he could take a picture.

He muttered a curse when he couldn't get the right angle. He'd have to hold the phone up too high, which would bring attention to his actions.

He'd have to walk by the men's table and try to get the picture. It would be tricky, and if he didn't get the photos on the first attempt, he wouldn't be able to do it at all. Walking by their table more than once was another sure way to attract their attention.

Liam asked the waitress where the bathroom was located and then made his move. As he passed by the table, he kept his phone on video-record mode. They would be able to pick up a still photo from the video. When he got to the bathroom he checked the footage. He'd gotten what he needed of one of the guys. As he walked back he'd get footage of the other one.

He waited a few moments before going out, but when he opened the door he realized the men were getting up to leave. He'd missed his chance for the second guy, damn it.

Keeping his head averted as they were paying, Liam threw a five-dollar bill down by his coffee cup and walked out the door. He needed to be back at his SUV before Webb left so they could continue to follow him.

It was beginning to rain in the darkness, which gave Liam an excuse to jog toward his car. His heart skipped a beat when he opened the door and realized Vanessa was no longer in the vehicle.

Adrenaline coursed through him. Where the hell had she gone? Had someone grabbed her? He was getting back out to look for her when the passenger door opened and she climbed in.

"Where were you?" Liam demanded.

"I could tell you only got pictures of one of the guys from the angle you were walking to the bathroom."

"So?" His heart was still beating a little too fast from thinking she had been taken.

"So, when I saw they were getting up to leave, I snuck to the window and took a picture of the other guy myself."

She was grinning like an idiot. Liam couldn't help smiling himself.

"I hope they didn't see you," he said, shaking his head.

"I don't think so," she said. "I kept to the shadows. If they did notice, they didn't act any differently."

"Here comes Webb." Liam started the SUV just as the assistant sheriff started his. "I think we should keep following him until we figure out who the other guys are."

He followed Webb at a safe distance. Enough people were leaving the diner that it wasn't too obvious they were following, but surveillance with only one car, at night, in a small place like the Outer Banks, was difficult. It wouldn't take long before Webb would become suspicious. Unless Webb was going out to the boat, following him wouldn't give them any sort of tactical advantage. If he was just going to his house, it wasn't worth the suspicions it would raise in Webb's mind.

Right now they were on the four-lane Highway 158. Everybody used that road, so it wouldn't grab Webb's attention.

"Getting out to take pictures of those guys could've been dangerous, you know," he said to Vanessa, who was straining to keep her eyes on Webb's car. "There's no doubt they're willing to kill to cover their tracks."

She shrugged. "No more dangerous than you going in there."

Liam gave a short laugh. "I'm a trained agent, not to mention I have nearly a foot and probably close to a hundred pounds on you."

She shrugged again. "It was worth the risk."

Liam had emailed the photos of both men to Omega as they'd waited at a stop light before moving on to the highway. Hopefully they would have positive IDs by morning, though Liam knew they couldn't be arrested or brought in for questioning. They would never give up the location of the girls;

it would be too incriminating against them. The girls would die alone on that boat.

Not an option.

But they could at least follow the men and put full-time surveillance on them.

Webb pulled off Highway 158 onto a smaller, darkened road. Things were about to get tricky.

Liam tossed Vanessa his phone. "Check the file with his info. Is his house on this road? If so, we don't want to follow. That will just make him suspicious."

She found the file quickly and her face jerked up to his. "No, his house is on the north side of the islands, near Kitty Hawk. Isn't this the road that leads out to the bridge to Riker's Island?"

She was right. An old wooden bridge that led out to a small island in the Sound the locals had nicknamed Riker's. The island was popular with young people during warm weather for lying out, sneaking a few illegal substances and just generally being young and stupid. Liam had spent time there himself as a teenager. A place to get away from endless tourists during the summer.

Right now, during the off season, it would be the perfect place to keep a small motor boat to get out to the bigger one where they were keeping the girls.

Liam switched off his headlights just before he turned onto the road leading out to the bridge. There was no way Webb wouldn't notice them behind him.

"If he gets in a boat, we don't have one," Vanessa reminded him.

"I know. We'll have to follow him as best we can with binoculars. It's better than nothing. Maybe they aren't far. Then we can come back out later tonight."

They kept a pretty good distance behind Webb. The island wasn't the only place these back roads led to, but it was a good bet. When Webb began slowing down, Liam stopped and backed up around a curb.

"I don't know if he sees us or what, but we need to stay out of sight for a minute. The last thing we want to do is spook him."

Of course, they didn't want to lose him, either. But if he was going to Riker's Island, that was a dead end.

Liam waited a full two minutes before easing the SUV around the bend again. He couldn't see Webb's taillights any longer.

They drove at a steady pace toward the bridge, slowing as they were about to ease onto it. Seeing the road without headlights was difficult.

"All right, let's see if the bastard went—"

He caught Vanessa's terrified look past him out the window as she threw out her arm toward him. He felt the jarring impact of another, much larger vehicle slamming into theirs.

Then everything went black.

Chapter Twelve

Why did she have her feet in cold water? Vanessa blinked, trying to wake all the way up.

Were they on a boat? They were rocking as though they were out on a boat.

She brought a hand to her head. Everything hurt. Was that blood on her hand? She couldn't see. And she couldn't really breathe because her seat belt was too tight.

As she blinked again and wiped her hair out of her face, her eyes adjusted.

Oh, God, she was in the car with Liam and they were *in the water*. The cold, salty water was already beginning to fill the vehicle. The windows were already below the water line.

How deep was the water here? Vanessa didn't know. But as the SUV continued to sink she realized it was deep enough to kill them.

She couldn't get a deep breath because so much

of her weight was being forced against her seat belt from the angle the vehicle was sinking.

And Liam was sitting there, still. Arms floating eerily from his angle in his seat.

He was too still. And whatever vehicle had hit them had connected on his side.

"Liam!" Vanessa yelled. She could now feel water inching up over her ankles.

He didn't move at all. She couldn't see any blood on him, but it was dark.

It was even darker in the water outside the windows.

She tried to reach over to touch him, but couldn't with the awkward angle her body was stuck in. She pushed at the release mechanism on her seat belt, panicking for just a second when it wouldn't give. Then it did and she fell forward.

The car shifted slightly with her movement. It was still filling with water.

"Liam," she yelled again, bracing herself against the dashboard so she could get closer to him. "Liam, wake up."

She shook his shoulder, then reached over and cupped both his cheeks with her hands.

"Liam, baby, I need you to wake up." She kissed him then patted his cheeks sharply.

The water was rising in the car. They were running out of time.

Liam moaned and she released a breath she hadn't even realized she'd been holding.

"That's right, you big old hunk of handsome. Wake up."

He groaned. "I prefer hunk of burning love."

Vanessa snickered and kissed him on the forehead. "I'll call you hunk of anything you want if we can get out of this vehicle alive."

It only took a moment for the cobwebs to clear in Liam's mind.

"We're already submerged. The water is rising inside the car." She could feel the cold creeping up toward her knees. The car was still sinking at an angle.

Liam reached for the controller to ease the window down, but it wouldn't work. "Electrical is already out."

Vanessa shrieked a little when the car hit the bottom and evened out. Her weight was thrown down into her seat.

Water was entering the car much faster now, pouring in through the floorboards.

"Okay, good, we're at the bottom," Liam said.

"That's good?"

He unhooked himself from his seat belt then took his gun out of his holster.

"Going to shoot some fish?" she asked. Maybe he could just shoot her. That would be a less painful way to go than drowning.

"No, I'm going to shoot your window out. Once the water fills the vehicle, we'll be able to swim out."

"Okay." It was a good plan in theory. "I don't know how far down we are. We were already sinking when I regained consciousness."

"Kick off your shoes," he said. "We're both good swimmers. We can make it."

She nodded but really wasn't sure.

"It might be disorienting when you first get through the window. You can't tell which way the surface is in the dark." He grabbed her hand. "If that happens, stop swimming and let yourself float for a second. You'll automatically start rising toward the surface. Then swim that way."

"Have you done this before?"

He reached over and kissed her. "Nah. But I was Houdini in another life."

She smiled. He'd always been able to make her smile, even in the craziest of circumstances or when she'd been so angry at him she was ready to hire a hit man.

He cupped her cheek. "The water coming in will be the hardest part. Don't panic, baby. We can't do anything until the car is full of water. The pressure of it coming in through the window will be too strong to swim against."

His eyes were serious.

Liam serious was frightening. She grasped his hand and squeezed.

"Cover your ears," he said as he pointed his gun at the window.

She did so, turning to the side. The sound of the

gun—shooting three times in rapid succession—
was so loud. But just as frightening was the sound
of the water now pouring in through the window.
The force of it tore through the holes the bullets
had made and ripped the window open like a gap-
ing wound.

Panic poured over Vanessa like the cold water.
Her breathing became shallow and tears pooled
in her eyes. Water was up to her waist in seconds.

"Nessa, look at me." He grabbed her hand in
the water. "Concentrate on your breathing. You're
going to need a deep breath before we swim up."

He breathed right in front of her. She tried to
follow his pattern, but the water was up to her
shoulders now.

"You can do this, baby. You're the strongest
person I know. The strongest person I've ever
known."

Vanessa focused. He was right, she *could* do
this. She had to do this or she would die. The
water now was just a few inches from the ceil-
ing of the car.

"One deep breath and then we swim, okay?"

"Okay," she said. They both had their heads
tilted straight up so they could get the last bit of
air. She heard him suck in a breath, then did the
same, her hand clutching his.

This was it.

Swimming, knowing you couldn't just pop up
for air if you needed it, was much different than

a regular swim. Vanessa had to force herself to remain calm. The pressing darkness all around her didn't help.

Liam swam through the window first. He had to let go of her to do so and she fought the panic once again. She couldn't see him at all.

Part of her shirt got caught on something as she took her turn through the window, so she just pulled on it with all her strength, causing it to rip. But at least it hurled her through the opening.

Where was Liam? Had he already gone toward the surface?

Which way was the surface?

She was running out of air and she hadn't even started swimming yet.

She remembered what he'd said about disorientation in the dark water. She tried to stop moving but couldn't tell which way her body was floating.

Now Vanessa really began to panic. She was at the last of her air. The overwhelming urge to gulp was almost unbearable, but she knew all she would get was water. And then she would drown.

She began to swim, because that was better than doing nothing, but she had no idea if she was heading toward the surface.

She felt a yank on her hair. Liam.

He kept a hand on her hair and reached out with the other one until he had hold of her hand. She was glad. She didn't want him to let go of her even for a second in this darkness. Together they swam.

Vanessa kept her breath as long as she could; the pressure became unbearable.

She held on another couple of seconds—fighting—but then couldn't any longer.

She opened her mouth and inhaled.

But instead of air, all she got was the painful sting of the brackish Sound water.

She couldn't fight the darkness anymore. Her last hope was that she didn't take Liam down with her as she drowned.

LIAM FELT VANESSA stop kicking a few feet from the surface. His own lungs burned with an agonizing intensity. He forced himself to give one more giant kick and their heads burst past the surface and into the life-giving air.

It only took him a moment to realize that Vanessa wasn't conscious. Wasn't breathing.

The vehicle had sunk father than he'd thought; probably nearly twenty feet. That was a long way to travel on one breath. Especially in Vanessa's panicked state.

He swam with her motionless form to the bank and pulled her up. Ignoring the cold that was making his movements sluggish, he tried to check her pulse. It was weak and thready, but it was still there. Pulse but no breath.

He had to get the water out of her system and air in or she wouldn't have a pulse soon. He turned her onto her side and thumped. Hard. She would have bruises on her small frame, no doubt.

"Come on, Nessa," he said, voice hoarse. "Stay with me."

He pulled her limp frame up, holding her with one arm across her chest, clasping her upper arm. He thumped again, leaning her forward as if burping a baby.

"Come on, sweetheart."

The sound of her retching was the most beautiful thing he'd ever heard.

He held her as she coughed and threw up the rest of the water in her system, replacing it with oxygen. Then he fell back onto the ground, taking her with him. They both lay exhausted.

"That wasn't fun," she finally whispered, obviously unable to make her voice any louder.

"Which part, the drowning or the epic vomiting?"

She chuckled weakly. "Both were equally gross."

Liam knew he had to get them up and going. The water had felt a lot colder than it actually was—it was only the first of October, so it wasn't dangerously cold—but they were both still freezing. They needed to warm up. Vanessa especially. She didn't have the same muscle mass he had to keep himself warm.

Whatever vehicle had pushed them into the water was gone. Could it have been Webb? Could he have seen them, doubled back and been waiting for them to make their way onto the bridge?

They'd have to figure that out later. Right now? Warmth. Of course, they had no vehicle, no working phones and no shoes. At least Liam still had his wallet.

He helped Vanessa up and they began walking. They'd head for the nearest hotel—thank God, the Outer Banks was fairly littered with them—get warm and call this in.

He kept Vanessa pinned to his side as they walked, slowly and pretty painfully, down the side road.

They were both alive. That was what mattered.

Chapter Thirteen

Vanessa's teeth were chattering and she was miserable.

If Liam reminded her one more time that shivering was a good sign, that it meant she hadn't gone into any later stages of hypothermia, she might pop him in the mouth. She didn't want to hear that the castanets playing in her head were a good sign. She just wanted to get warm.

They hadn't had to walk far for a hotel, thank goodness. He had kept her pinned to his side the entire time except when he'd reluctantly let her go so he could check in. Vanessa sat outside on a bench waiting, since they both looked like something out of *The Creature from the Black Lagoon*. Plus, he didn't want the clerk to possibly recognize her in case the cops started searching again.

Even in her physical misery, Vanessa couldn't ignore the overwhelming joy that permeated her body.

They were alive.

Both of them were walking, no broken bones, no obvious head injuries, no floating facedown in the Roanoke Sound. They had some cuts and definitely some bruises, but they were *alive*.

Liam walked back outside. "Okay, I've got us a room and extra bottles of shampoo and conditioner."

This hotel was pretty nice. Not luxury, like something her family would stay at, but certainly not as scary as the other place she'd been with Karine. Liam led her inside, into the elevator and up to their room. He immediately went to the heating unit and cranked it to high.

Vanessa wanted to fall face-first on the giant king-size bed, but definitely needed a shower first.

She wondered if she could talk Liam into joining her. That would warm both of them up. She looked over at him, but he was already grabbing the phone and stretching it over to the table by the window.

"I'm going to make a call to Omega Sector," he said. "Make sure we have backup on the way and that they are bringing everything we need."

She knew she should be happy that he was in super-agent mode. He was getting things done. Making sure those girls were going to make it out of this situation alive. Calling in the guard.

Was it bad that she wished—just a little bit—he would be in let's-celebrate-we're-alive mode and join her in the shower?

Probably.

"Do you think that was Webb who rammed us into the water tonight?" she asked him.

He nodded. "Maybe. Him or one of his friends. They could've noticed we were following him."

"It's a good thing we sent those pictures already. My phone didn't make it out of the Sound."

"Mine did, but it's completely useless. We'll need to get replacements tomorrow. And figure out a plan about everything. I'm thinking the best bet is for you to go to work as if nothing happened. That would completely throw Webb, or whoever tried to kill us, off."

"Won't he just bring me in again?"

"Not with your dad's lawyer there to get you out. I know you don't like your dad's interference, but nobody is going to bring you in for questioning unless they are absolutely sure they can charge you with something. The Epperson lawyer made sure of that, I have no doubt." He turned back to the phone.

Yeah, Liam was definitely in super-agent mode. That was good, she reminded herself. Good.

She spun and made her way to the shower, by herself.

Good.

LIAM CATEGORICALLY REFUSED to think about Vanessa in the shower as he made his calls. First one was to Andrea to check on Karine and to make sure she knew to be even more diligent. Andrea assured him everything was okay there.

He knew Vanessa—who was not being thought of naked in the shower—would be glad to know everything was fine on the home front.

His next call was to Omega, reporting to Steve Drackett about the attack. It didn't change much. Derek and Joe would be in the Outer Banks tomorrow morning. They hadn't had any luck identifying the men Liam and Vanessa had sent pictures of, but the facial recognition software was still running them.

Of course, facial recognition programming was limited. Unless the men had a record or were public figures, the software might not come up with any helpful results.

By the time Liam got off the phone with Steve, the shower had stopped. At least now he could stop not thinking about Vanessa naked in the shower.

And while he was not thinking about things, he definitely should not think about that explosive kiss between them this morning before she'd gone to work. How he'd dragged her across his lap and every window in the vehicle had fogged in under ten seconds.

The bathroom door opened and she stepped out, wrapped only in a towel.

Add that to the don't-think-about list, also.

"It's all yours. I rinsed out my clothes because

they were so gross with the Sound water. They're on the sink."

Liam looked everywhere but at her. "Okay. I don't blame you."

"Everything okay with Karine and Andrea?"

"Yes, no problems whatsoever." He glanced over at her, drawn by the expanse of her shoulders not covered by the towel, then quickly away. "Andrea is on high alert, but I don't think they can tie anything having to do with you and me to her, even if they know who I am, which is doubtful. So they're safe."

He glanced at her to gauge her reaction, but was instead transfixed by a drop of water that found its way from the damp hair at her temple down her cheek and neck. It moved on to her chest, only to disappear in the track between her breasts.

All Liam could think about was backing Vanessa up against that wall and following with his lips the same path that droplet had taken.

Of untying that towel wrapped around her and letting it drop to the floor. And following the routes a few more droplets of water had taken down her body, or just make up his own.

Damn, he was not supposed to be thinking of any of this.

"I'm going to shower." He didn't look Vanessa in the face; just went into the bathroom.

That was what he needed: a little distance, a nice hot shower to wipe out the lingering cold and salt clinging to his skin; time to just let everything that had happened today go.

Five minutes into his shower, he realized it wasn't going to help at all.

The more he tried not thinking about Vanessa—naked, fully clothed or otherwise—the more he couldn't get her out of his mind. He was going to have to get another room. That was the only way he'd be able to leave her alone.

He didn't rinse out his clothes, but put them back on grudgingly, wincing at their stiffness and smell. He needed to go down to the lobby to ask for a second room. He stepped out of the bathroom still drying his hair with a towel.

"Hey, Nessa, I was thinking. It would probably be prudent for me to get my own—"

He looked up from under his towel and halted his words. Vanessa was lying on the bed, under the covers, curled up in a ball. She was fast asleep.

"Room," Liam finished in a much softer voice.

It would probably still be prudent. But Liam had never been particularly good at prudent.

Besides, he trusted himself not to molest a sleeping woman. Even if she was the most gorgeous, feminine, sexy woman he'd ever known.

Liam went back into the bathroom and rinsed out his clothes. He laid them next to Vanessa's to dry then turned out the lights. He got into the bed, moving carefully so he wouldn't wake her.

So he was quite surprised when, a few seconds later, a very naked Vanessa pressed up to his side.

"I tricked you," she said, giggling, then covered her mouth as if she was surprised at the sound.

That sweet laugh. Lord, how he had missed it. He hadn't realized until right now that Vanessa's infectious laughter was probably what he had missed most about her over the past eight years.

He hadn't heard it once since he was back, until now. Sure, circumstances were dire, he knew that, but it was almost as if that sweet laugh wasn't part of Vanessa's regular makeup anymore. More than ever, he was determined to understand what had changed for her. What had made her stop laughing?

But he'd have to worry about that later. Right now it looked as though the laughing Vanessa had other plans.

The time for prudence had come and gone. Liam could hardly fight his own desires. There was no way in hell he could fight his *and* hers.

He turned onto his side so they were face to face and wrapped an arm around her, pulling her closer. "You certainly had me fooled, Miss Epperson."

"I had to get you out of super-agent mode. This seemed like the easiest way."

Liam cocked an eyebrow. "Super-agent mode?"

She rubbed a hand over his chest. "Yeah. I didn't need an agent. I need Liam."

"Well, he's here now."

He pulled Vanessa so she lay all the way on top

of him. The thought that he could have lost her today—had come so close to losing her—had him crushing her to him. He wrapped one arm around her hips and threaded his other hand through her hair, bringing her lips down to his.

The heat was instantaneous, as always. It chased all traces of cold away.

"I thought I'd lost you tonight," he murmured against her lips.

"I had the same fear when I couldn't get you to wake up in the car," she responded, her lips never moving away from his.

There was no more talking. Neither of them wanted to think about death. Not right now. Liam didn't want to even think about whether this was a good idea or not.

All he wanted to think about was her body pressed up against his.

He rolled them over so she was tucked underneath him, catching his weight on his elbow and using his other hand to run down the length of her body. He heard her breath catch as he became reunited with the body he had once known so well.

She reached up and threaded her hands in his hair, pulling his lips down to hers. He got one last glimpse of the endless brown in her eyes before he closed his and gave himself over to the passion between them.

As if they'd never been apart.

Chapter Fourteen

Liam was hard-pressed to remember a time he'd been as relieved to see anyone as he was to see his fellow Omega agents Derek Waterman and Joe Matarazzo the next day. Without them Liam's focus had been too torn: trying to make sure Vanessa was safe at work, getting some sense of where Tommy Webb was and what he was doing, plus keeping an eye out for either of the two men he'd been with, since the facial-recognition software still hadn't netted any results.

It was too much for any one person.

Now Liam had the backup he needed. He trusted these men in a way he didn't trust anyone else. He'd learned how to put his life in other people's hands when he'd entered the army and then qualified for Special Forces. His multiple direct-action missions in Afghanistan had taught him the very essence of teamwork. He'd thought the camaraderie would be gone forever after he'd left

Special Forces, but he'd found the same brother-hood at Omega Sector.

Of course, right now they were giving him a hard time and he wished he wasn't stuck with them.

"Are we certain it wasn't one of Goetz's ex-girlfriends who rammed him off the bridge?" Joe asked, stretched out in the backseat of Liam's new rental car.

Derek, sitting next to Liam in the front, shook his head. "Joe, you need to be serious."

Liam nodded. "Thanks, Derek."

"We all know there is not enough law-enforce-ment manpower in the world to track down all the women who would like to run Liam off a bridge," Derek continued, causing Joe to chuckle. "We'll have to just hope it's some criminal. Then we have a chance."

"Very funny," Liam muttered. Although Liam guessed he deserved it after how much he had teased Derek about his wife, Molly, the forensic lab director at Omega.

They had already inspected Webb's vehicle, at least the one he'd been driving last night, which he had parked at the station today. There was no damage to the front of his car. It could not have been the vehicle that had pushed them off the bridge.

That didn't mean it hadn't been one of his bud-dies, though.

"I'm going to leave you two comedians here to watch Webb. Particularly to see if he meets up with our unknown suspects again." Both Joe and Derek had the pictures he and Vanessa had taken at the diner and they each had a car in case they needed to split up.

Liam had also gotten new phones for him and Vanessa. Being out of touch was not an option.

"I should probably check in with Andrea, make sure everything is okay there. I don't want to take Vanessa to that house in case someone is following us. Webb might have surveillance on her that we don't know about."

Joe looked at him, all joking now aside. "You need to be careful out there, man. Whoever is behind this is hard-core."

Liam nodded. "I'm just hoping those girls are still alive and the perps haven't moved up their timetable. We need to watch them, but nothing that will arouse unwanted suspicion."

"Let's just hope they're more greedy than they are smart," Derek said. "They won't want to lose the money those girls will provide unless they absolutely have to."

"I'm going to stick with Vanessa. They couldn't get her out of the way through legal channels, so now it looks like they're trying to get rid of her altogether."

There was no way Liam would be leaving her

side once she was out of her office, in case whoever had tried to kill them yesterday decided to come back and finish the job while Vanessa was alone.

That decision, of course, had nothing to do with the lovemaking that had occurred last night. And this morning. Twice.

It was Friday afternoon and Vanessa would be done with work soon. He wouldn't have to let her out of his sight all weekend. He wished he could keep her naked that whole time, but knew they had work to do.

Plus, what the hell was he doing? He had come here to the Outer Banks to put Vanessa's ghost to rest. To finally be able to move on without the thought of her hanging over every action he made.

That definitely was a mission fail.

As he waited outside her office—still not completely able to wrap his head around the fact that Vanessa was a social worker—Liam knew he had to face some hard facts.

He had never really gotten over Vanessa.

The situation had just become a great deal more complicated based on last night's—and this morning's—actions.

Vanessa was not the same person he'd known eight years ago. Of course, he wasn't the same person, either. They'd both grown up. But something had changed her. She didn't want to share it, but before he left this place, Liam was going to know what it was.

And how was he going to leave her again? He'd barely survived leaving her once. And that was because he'd been forced to. But even if they could work out their differences, her life was here and his was in Colorado.

There was one thing he had better remember and consider more than anything else: he had been in this exact place before. Eight years ago. Sitting there making future plans for him and Vanessa. Sure that all the love and heat and passion between them was two-sided.

Then she had just up and changed her mind.

How stupid would he be to allow the exact same thing to happen? Yeah, they'd had sex, but she'd given him no indication that there was anything permanent between them.

Hell, even when she *had* promised him things were permanent between them, she hadn't meant it. How much less so now when she wasn't making any promises at all?

He would be best served by keeping that forefront in his mind.

He was here to exorcise her ghost. Maybe a few rolls in the hay were necessary to accomplish that mission. But his heart needed to stay *way* out of it.

Liam saw Vanessa coming out the office door and shut down his thoughts. He usually wasn't one to sit around overthinking things. Liam preferred action.

Unfortunately this time he wasn't sure what action to take.

IT HAD BEEN a pretty damn stressful day at work.

First, she'd had to wear the same clothes—again—except this time they were even worse because they'd been in salty water and even rinsing them thoroughly at the hotel hadn't gotten them completely clean.

Not to mention Vanessa had arrived utterly exhausted this morning. Sure, a lot of that had been from the absolutely fabulous bouts of lovemaking between her and Liam. But the exhaustion had also stemmed from almost being killed and spending half the day being questioned by the police.

Her body had had enough.

Her boss, Maureen, had wanted answers as soon as Vanessa walked through the door. Why had she been taken by the police? Why was she being questioned? Did any of this have to do with any of her cases? Did she really think it was a good example if any of the families she worked with had seen her being marched down to the sheriff's office?

Vanessa hadn't been able to easily defend herself, since telling the truth wasn't an option. So in the end Maureen had thought it better if Vanessa take a leave of absence until things were more settled. She would review and make a final decision about Vanessa's continued employment at Bridge-span once all the facts were available.

Vanessa had spent the rest of the day phoning some families she worked closely with to let them know she wouldn't be around for a while. She used the excuse of a family emergency. Seemed fitting.

She also spent a few hours going over her cases with other counselors in her office. Vanessa wasn't sure how long this nonsense with the sheriff's office was going to drag out and she wanted to make sure her families were taken care of in the meantime.

All her colleagues were wary of her. They didn't say anything outright, but Vanessa could tell. After all, it wasn't every day not one but two uniformed officers came and escorted someone out of the office. Especially not an Epperson.

And then, as the long day finally finished, she went out to the car ready to see a friendly face—*Liam's* friendly face—but instead he'd been cool and reserved. Maybe he'd just been in super-agent mode again, but it still had stung. They had decided she should drive her car home and he would follow her in the new rental. She was no longer trying to stay away from her apartment now that Karine was with Andrea at a different location.

So now here they were, parked and walking up the stairs to her second-floor unit. He was only a couple feet behind her, but the chasm between them seemed huge to Vanessa.

Sadly, she didn't know Liam well enough anymore to know what was causing the distance. Was this just how he did his job? She could understand if he didn't want to be focused on her if he was trying to see if they were being watched or whatever.

Did he regret last night? Resent that she'd tricked him into getting into bed? She'd meant it in a lighthearted fashion, and he seemed to have taken it that way, but now she didn't know. He'd seemed fine this morning but hadn't touched her since she'd gotten off work.

He did finally touch her as she took the key out to open her apartment door. He touched her hand to take it from her.

"I'm going to go in and check it out first, just in case."

She stepped back as he drew his gun out of the holster under his jacket. She knew he carried a weapon, but still wasn't used to seeing it up close and personal. She hadn't even thought about checking her apartment before going in.

"Stay here," he said.

He was inside the door, weapon raised, before she could even respond. She watched from the entrance as he looked around corners and in closets. It didn't take him long to search her apartment—the two-bedroom, one-bath place wasn't very big—and he came back out, gun out of sight.

"Okay, all clear." He stood to the side so she could come through the door.

Still very much not touching her.

She stepped through, closed the door behind her and walked into the kitchen.

Maybe something had happened today that she didn't know about. His colleagues had arrived, she knew from the text he'd sent her. She now had their numbers in her phone as well as Andrea's and Karine's—although Karine's was just listed in her contacts under "Kay."

Maybe he had bad news and didn't want to tell her. Some info about the men they'd seen with Webb. Or, God forbid, the girls.

She turned to him, reaching out to touch his arm on the biceps. She stroked softly. "Is everything okay? Anything bad happen today?"

For just a second he leaned into her touch. She slid that hand up to his shoulder and reached her other arm up to the other shoulder, too, pulling him to her, even as she stepped toward him.

She thought for a moment he would meet her in the embrace, but instead he stiffened and pulled away.

"Everything's fine." He took another small step back. "I just want to get those girls out, that's all."

Vanessa didn't want to nag, didn't want to pressure him into talking if he didn't want to. But this tension around them was hard. She didn't like it and wanted to ease it if she could. She took another step toward him.

"Are you sure that's it? You seem…" She searched for the right word. Mad. Cold. "Distant. After last night, I just want to make sure everything is okay with us."

She smiled and reached for him.

His icy look stopped her. "You mean being concerned about the lives of seven young girls is not enough? Maybe you need to quit assuming the world revolves around you."

Chapter Fifteen

She tried not to show how his words hurt her. "I'm going to take a shower."

Vanessa turned and walked out of the kitchen. Her voice didn't shake. She didn't cry. Her shoulders and head were high. Hell, she'd had enough years of being an Epperson to know how to look as though she was in control no matter what.

But inside she could actually feel her heart crack. Once she was around the corner, she began rubbing her chest as if that would ease a pain that wasn't physical.

Liam still thought of her as a selfish, self-centered person. He all but hated her.

She walked into the bathroom, shut the door behind her and peeled off yesterday's offensive clothes. The dried salt dragged across her skin like sandpaper as she removed them.

He didn't hate her. That was melodramatic. But

he sure as hell wasn't interested in being close to her.

Liam Goetz hadn't been a part of her life in eight years. It shouldn't affect her at all if he wasn't interested in being a part of her life now.

But it did. She felt the tears she couldn't fight anymore well up in her eyes as she opened the door and stepped into the shower. His words had sliced at her.

Especially after the past twenty-four hours. She didn't think their lovemaking had erased all the pain from their past—nothing could do that—but she hadn't thought it was just physical. It had been hot and passionate and something more.

At least it had been for her.

Evidently it had just been an opportunity too good to pass up for him. Just sex. Whatever anger he'd had for her eight years ago he obviously still had now.

As if he had the right to be angry. He hadn't lost everything.

She tried to hold on to that thought, to hold on to the anger and let it push out the pain, but she couldn't. The look in Liam's eyes in the kitchen was inescapable in her mind. More tears fell at the thought of it. He regretted last night. Maybe not the physical act itself, but he regretted their intimacy. And he still thought her selfish and self-centered.

Some things never changed.

She was startled to see the door to the shower stall open. Liam stood there, fully dressed. He reached over and shut off the water.

"I'm an idiot. I'm sorry," he said.

Vanessa stood there, dripping. He didn't look anywhere but at her face. In her eyes. She thought she could see actual anguish in his.

It was hard to look at him. "You said what you felt. You weren't very gentle about it, but you shouldn't apologize for saying what you think is the truth."

"But that's it. It's not what I think is the truth."

He took a towel hanging on the rack next to him. She expected him to hand it to her, but instead he wrapped it over her head and began to gently dry her hair.

"You've always thought I was spoiled, Liam. Self-entitled."

His fingers gripped the wet ends of her hair with the towel. "You were young. Your family had gobs of money. You usually got what you wanted. But even then you weren't spoiled. Weren't ever mean."

He left that towel on her head and grabbed another one and began drying her body, starting with her neck and shoulders. Vanessa wasn't sure what to do so she just stood there.

"And you definitely aren't spoiled now. You are the opposite of self-centered."

"But in the kitchen—"

"In the kitchen I was a moron." She closed her eyes as he dried his way down her torso slowly and firmly. "I let frustration from the case, frustration from our past, bubble up into where we are now. I'm sorry."

"About last night—"

He crouched and began to dry her feet, slowly working his way up her legs. "Last night and this morning were incredible. I was just having a little difficulty separating the past from the present."

She gasped softly as he dried all the way up her thighs.

You need to tell him everything.

She pushed the thought away as he stood and wrapped the towel around her waist, drying her back and buttocks. He grabbed the towel on both sides and wrapped the edges around his fists to drag her closer. He put his head down so his forehead touched hers.

"I'm an idiot. I'm sorry." He echoed the same words he'd started the conversation with. "Come to bed with me and let me make it up to you."

She tilted up her face to tell him his apology wasn't necessary, but he captured her lips in a kiss as he pulled her hips closer with the towel. The heat was there instantly, as always. As his tongue met hers, she forgot to breathe. Forgot everything but this feeling that had always existed between them. Eight years hadn't erased it.

He reached down and scooped her up, towels

and all. He carried her to the bedroom and lay her down gently, reverently.

And proceeded to more than make up for it.

AFTERWARD THEY BOTH fell into an exhausted sleep. Their bodies didn't give them any other option. The pink light of dawn was creeping through her bedroom window when Vanessa finally peeled her eyes open.

Liam was lying on his side against her, face pressed to her neck, his arm and leg draped over her. She couldn't escape now if she wanted to.

She didn't want to.

She had never wanted to.

She needed to tell him the truth about eight years ago. It wouldn't change anything—nothing could change what had happened—but he deserved to know.

She felt him begin to stir. If she didn't tell him now, she'd never do it.

"I never chose my family, or my wealthy lifestyle, or whatever you want to call it, over you." Her voice was soft, husky with sleep, but she knew he heard her. As close as they were, she could feel the tension creep into his body.

"I don't understand. I came to your house. I heard you tell your family you didn't want to see anyone."

At least he was still lying against her. She just

needed to get it out. "You asked me to marry you on September twelfth."

"I remember." His voice was strained.

"Do you? Do you really remember that day?" she asked.

They'd been on the beach walking. He'd gotten out of the army a few months prior and had started a job at the Drug Enforcement Agency—brought in as an agent because of his experience in Special Forces. He hadn't been exactly sure where they would be sending him, but he knew it would be Philadelphia, Chicago or Salt Lake City.

Wherever it was, he'd wanted Vanessa to come with him.

They'd been apart too much for the four years he was in the army, only seeing each other when he could make it home on leave. And even then they'd had to sneak around if they'd wanted any intimate time with each other. Vanessa had just barely turned twenty and still lived at home.

He'd asked her to marry him—to go to Vegas or a justice of the peace—so it could be done quickly. Both of them knew her parents would never give their blessing. So Vanessa and Liam wouldn't ask for their blessing. They would just do it.

He would come back for her a month later. She had agreed to be ready and to meet him there at the beach with whatever she needed to bring.

The relief Vanessa had felt that he'd asked her to marry him was high. She'd had news of her own to tell him but hadn't known how to say it. His proposal had taken off a lot of the pressure.

"Do you remember my reaction when you asked me to marry you?" she said.

More tension. "Joy, I thought," he said. "I thought you were as excited about it as I was."

"Anything else?"

He stayed against her for a long minute. "I don't know." He finally shrugged. "You seemed a little distracted or something, but I thought it had to do with all the planning and maybe fear about your parents. I definitely remember the fact that you wouldn't let me make love to you on the beach."

Vanessa closed her eyes and nodded. This was it. "Because I was young, and didn't know anything. And I was afraid having sex might hurt the baby," she whispered.

She knew the exact second her words sank in. He jerked away from her and was sitting up in less than a second flat.

"What?"

"That's why I was distracted that day. I had just found out I was pregnant the day before."

Myriad emotions crossed his face. "You were pregnant?"

"From when you had been home on leave six weeks before."

He still stared at her, mouth agape.

"I wasn't sure how to tell you," she continued. "I knew the job with the DEA was a big thing, and

I wasn't sure exactly what our plans would be…if a baby would even fit into the plans."

She rushed on before he could say anything. "But then you asked me to marry you. You had to leave that night and things were crazy. I thought I would just tell you once you came back for me. We would figure it out together."

He blinked rapidly. "I don't understand."

Vanessa closed her eyes and took a deep breath. She had to get through this without breaking down.

"I went to a doctor to make sure everything was okay and someone at the office tipped off my parents." She opened her eyes. "They found out about the baby two days before you were supposed to come back. I told them I was leaving with you. That we were getting married."

Vanessa could feel the tears welling, but she forced them back. If she let herself start crying now, she'd never get through this. "My parents and I fought. I walked a few steps down our big staircase and then turned to yell some smart-aleck remark back up at them."

"Nessa—"

"I tripped. I fell all the way down."

Vanessa couldn't remember much about the fall. She remembered a sharp pain in her midsection before everything went black.

She looked over at Liam, who was staring at her

as if he could barely comprehend what she was saying. She knew this was a lot to take in.

"They took me to the hospital. I lost the baby." Her throat closed up and the words came out as barely more than a squeak.

"Oh, my God, Nessa." Liam ran a hand over his face. "Why didn't you tell me? Why didn't you call right away?"

"I was sedated at the hospital when they did an emergency D & C to keep anything from rupturing."

"Of course. I understand that. I would've understood it then, too. I would've been there."

"I came home the next day, but I was so out of it, Liam. I didn't know what day it was. I was distraught. My parents' doctor continued to keep me on drugs."

She saw realization dawn on his face. "When you didn't meet me at the beach like you were supposed to, I came to your parents' house. You were still under sedation when I got there."

"Yes. But, in their defense, I was hysterical. I wasn't handling anything well. Sobbing uncontrollably for hours."

Liam closed his eyes. Every nuance of his expression bespoke pain.

"When your father said you weren't going anywhere, that you'd changed your mind about everything, I didn't believe him. But when I heard you say you didn't want to see me, I thought he must have been telling the truth. You said you didn't want to see me—*to make me leave*."

She couldn't stop the tears. "It's all very blurry to me, but the one thought I kept having was that I didn't know how to tell you. I had miscarried our baby, Liam, from my own stupidity. I didn't want to tell you. So the words you heard were probably true."

He shook his head, wiping a hand across his face again, wearily.

"But I never meant I didn't want to marry you," Vanessa continued. "My dad knew that and deliberately misled you. Once I began to come around, to realize I hadn't seen you, it was too late. It was days past when we were supposed to meet. My dad didn't tell me you'd come by, or what he'd said, until much later."

They both sat looking at each other in silence. The past lay between them like a canyon.

Vanessa finally spoke. "What my parents did was unforgivable. Once I found out, I walked away from them without looking back. But you had also walked away without looking back."

Chapter Sixteen

Liam felt as if he had been hit by a truck. The so-called facts that had shaped every detail of his life for the past eight years had just been proved false with one relatively brief conversation.

He couldn't sit on the bed any longer. Too much energy was coursing through him. He was still naked, so he grabbed his boxers from the floor and put them on.

He wanted to punch a wall, to fight an unseen foe, to howl out his pain. For a barely twenty-year-old Vanessa who had lost their baby. For himself at twenty-two thinking the love of his life had left him cold.

For all the years that had been lost. The pain both of them had lived through.

"Why didn't you tell me, Nessa?" he whispered, stopping his pacing. "Find me and make me understand?"

"After I left my parents I looked for you, but

you were gone. I called that phone number you'd given me with the DEA, but they said you were unavailable. I tracked down your buddies here on the island a few days later, like I told you, hoping you were still on the Outer Banks. They told me what you'd said."

"Vanessa Epperson will never be anything but a selfish, spoiled brat who doesn't have it in her to care about another person." Liam remembered what he'd said. And at the time he had meant every word.

She shrugged. "That, combined with what had just happened, was too much for me. I pretty much shut down."

Liam walked over to the window and looked out. It was a terrible view of a parking lot and Dumpster, a testament of the modest rent of the apartment complex.

"Not that it makes a difference now, but when you called the DEA, I was on a deep undercover operation in Chicago. They didn't usually put someone so new under right away, but they'd needed someone young, rough around the edges and with nothing to lose, to go in immediate under pretty dire circumstances. I fit the bill to a tee."

He didn't tell her that he'd nearly died in that mission. He'd stayed in deep cover for six months, and when the DEA made its move against the drug ring he'd infiltrated, there had been such a shoot-out that he'd ended up in the hospital with two gunshot wounds.

He turned back to glance at her. "The DEA wouldn't have provided any info about me to you, of course. They didn't tell me of any messages."

"I didn't leave one," she whispered.

"And you've been away from your family ever since? Even though I know they didn't approve of me, I know you guys were so close."

She sat upright against the headboard of her bed and brought her knees to her chest under the sheet. She wrapped her arms around them. "I just couldn't stay there. I couldn't look at them the same ever again after that. I know the miscarriage wasn't their fault, but I just couldn't forgive them for chasing you away."

He pressed his forehead against the coolness of the window. "I should've come back to check on you. To fight for you. For us."

He hadn't been able to because of his mission.

But he wouldn't have anyway, even if his job at the DEA hadn't prohibited it. Because he'd always believed, deep inside, that the poor, orphaned kid—who'd been in trouble with the law—being raised by his grandmother, wasn't good enough for Vanessa Epperson, Princess of the Outer Banks.

Somewhere in his mind he'd always known it was just a matter of time before she figured it out, too. So when her parents had stood there and told him it had finally happened—that she'd come to her senses and realized he could never provide for her the way she would want to be provided for—it was just what he'd always expected.

And while he'd never really believed those harsh things he'd said to his friends—he'd been so angry and hurt at the time—he had to admit he had wondered, *worried*, if she could live without the pampering she'd been so used to.

How wrong he'd been. This tiny apartment—with a view of a Dumpster, for God's sake—was proof of that. That piece of junk car she drove, another. She not only could live without it, she had been choosing to live without it of her own accord for nearly a decade.

He shook his head. "I never should've said that to my friends. Whether I believed it or not, I never should have said it," he said without looking at her.

"I was spoiled."

Now he turned. "You were *loved*. Pampered, but not spoiled. You never thought of yourself as better than others or that your money entitled you to things other people couldn't have."

Her arms were still wrapped around her knees as if she were trying to keep the pieces from flying apart. That look, that sadness he'd recognized the first day he'd seen her, was back. At least now he understood what it meant.

She'd lost a child.

They'd lost a child.

Liam had no doubt it would've been loved—

a little boy or girl. But having a child so early on would've changed the course of his life. He doubted he would be employed at Omega right now or would've shot so high in the ranks at the DEA.

Liam would've given the career stuff up in a heartbeat to have had Vanessa—and their child— healthy and happy and with him.

He was a man of action. A guy who got things done, often by any means necessary. It made him very effective at hostage rescue.

But there was no action he could take now, nothing that could ever be done, that would erase the desperate sadness that sometimes crept into Vanessa's eyes.

Too many years had passed, and even though they had just spent the night wrapped in each other's arms, the emotional chasm between them felt too large to ever be fully bridged.

Liam could never make up for the time lost. He felt a heavy weight on his shoulders. What could he do?

He, the man of action, couldn't figure out any action to take.

"Liam—"

A pounding on the front door stopped them.

Liam glanced at his watch. "Expecting anybody at seven o'clock on a Saturday morning?"

"No. Definitely not."

Liam snatched up his weapon from where he'd

set the holster on the chair in the living room last night before going in to apologize to her in the shower.

He slipped on his jeans and she grabbed a robe. They walked to the front door. Vanessa cracked it open just the slightest bit.

It was Tommy Webb.

"Where's Liam Goetz?" the man asked without any sort of greeting. "He needs to come down to the sheriff's office to answer some questions."

Liam stuck his head in front of the crack so Webb could see him. "I'm right here. What do you want?" He kept his weapon down at his leg where the assistant sheriff wouldn't notice it.

"Someone saw the two of you together and recognized you. I understand you had quite the run-ins with the law when you lived here before. I have some questions for you."

"Fine," Liam said. "I need a couple minutes to get dressed."

"Be warned, I have a man planted at the back of the complex, too. So don't try to run."

Liam rolled his eyes. "I'm not going to jump from a second-story balcony to get away from you just because you have *questions*. I'll be out in a few minutes."

"Hurry up."

Liam shut the door.

"What are we going to do?" Vanessa asked.

"I'm going to go with him."

"What?"

"He doesn't know that I'm law enforcement. At a cursory glance, because of some of the undercover work I've done, my employment with Omega or the DEA doesn't show up in a background check. I don't work undercover anymore, so my info is in all law-enforcement networks, but you have to dig a little further to find it."

"Are you sure?"

"He wouldn't be here like this if he knew I was law enforcement. He just thinks I'm a punk with a record who has shown up at a pretty inconvenient time."

Liam got dressed in fresh jeans and a black T-shirt.

"Why does he want to question you if he's the one involved with the trafficking ring?"

Liam wasn't sure about that. "I don't know. Maybe my connection to you. To see if there are holes in our story about Karine."

He slipped on his tennis shoes and sat to tie them. "I'm going to text Derek and Joe. Stay here and don't go anywhere with anyone except them. One of them will be here within fifteen minutes."

Her face was worried. He wished he could reassure her.

"Should I call my dad and get him to send his lawyer?"

Liam knew how much it cost her to ask that. He

sent his text to Derek and walked over to stand right in front of her. He tucked her hair behind both ears on either side of her face and left his hands on her cheeks.

"I'm going to be fine. This is actually a good thing," he said. "It gives me a chance to size up Webb. He thinks he's questioning me, but I'm going to be doing some delving of my own."

She nodded but didn't look too convinced. He reached down and kissed her gently. "I wish I could stay with you. I don't want to leave you now, especially not after our talk. Are you okay?"

Webb knocked on the door again. "Let's go, Goetz," he called.

Liam ignored him, all his focus on Vanessa.

She nodded. "Yeah, I'm okay. Just worried about you."

Liam's phone chirped with a message from Derek. Joe was only five minutes from Vanessa's apartment and would be there shortly.

That reassured Liam. After the near-drowning episode, he was loath to leave her alone. He kissed her again.

"Joe Matarazzo will be here any minute. He's an Omega agent, too. One of the best. Don't let him charm you into doing something stupid."

Vanessa raised one eyebrow. "I make no promises."

Liam chuckled and kissed her again. "I'll let you know as soon as I'm out."

"Be careful. You don't know who you can trust."

Liam turned and opened the door to Tommy Webb. He was very aware of that fact.

Chapter Seventeen

Webb started with the questions Liam had been expecting. How he knew Vanessa. His history with the police. Where he and Vanessa had been this week. If he knew anything about a teenage runaway sought for multiple crimes.

Webb showed him the footage of the break-in turned murder. Looking at it, knowing it couldn't possibly be Karine because she'd been with them on Tuesday night, Liam could easily see the setup.

Long brown hair evident throughout the clip. A slightly blurred image of Karine's face superimposed over whoever the person was in the video.

But it was a damn good job, Liam had to admit.

The questions took more than an hour. Webb would come at him from one angle and then another, hoping to catch Liam in a lie or a statement that contradicted what Vanessa had told them.

It was nothing more than a fishing expedition. Webb didn't have any real information about anything, partially because neither Liam nor Vanessa had done anything wrong.

But part of it was something else. As though Webb really was trying to get to the bottom of something he didn't quite understand. That he knew something was wrong but didn't know what.

Liam decided to take a chance.

Up until now Liam had been playing the bored hard-ass when answering Webb's questions— leaning back in his chair, focusing on his fingernails or an invisible spot on the leg of his jeans. But he stepped out of his role for a minute and really looked at the young assistant sheriff.

Webb was startled by Liam's sudden intensity as Liam leaned forward and put his weight on his forearms on the table between them.

"Webb, why are we here at this ungodly hour on a Saturday morning?"

Webb was taken aback by the question. "What do you mean? I'm trying to solve a murder. That's my job, Goetz. I'm the assistant sheriff of—"

Liam didn't let him finish his tirade. "And has there been anything odd about this particular murder, Webb? Stuff that just isn't adding up?"

Liam realized he was taking a pretty big chance. But if his instincts were correct, then they'd been wrong and Webb wasn't the person involved with the trafficking ring.

Webb looked at Liam for a long moment. "What sort of stuff?"

So the man *was* suspicious.

Liam shrugged. "I'm not sure exactly. Things just not adding up the way you think they should."

"Do you know something I need to know about?"

Liam turned and glanced at the two-way mirror behind him. He had no idea who was listening in on this conversation. Even if Webb wasn't their guy, it was someone from this office, and that person could be listening. Liam couldn't mention Karine or the girls.

On the other hand, if Webb was what Liam thought he was—an overzealous cop with political ambitions trying to make a name for himself and get some publicity by solving a murder—he could be an excellent ally.

"Webb, go see who's in the observation room."

"Why?"

"Just do it."

Webb shook his head but got up and left the interview room. A few moments later he was back.

"There's nobody in there," Webb said. "It's barely eight o'clock on a Saturday morning. Unless people have to be here, they're at home."

When Webb sat, Liam leaned forward and spoke as softly as he could.

"Somebody is going to figure out you have me

here. I don't know who, but whoever that person is, you need to watch him, Webb. Carefully."

"What the hell are you talking about?"

"Did someone tell you to bring me in for questioning?"

"No. I figured out who you were and brought you in myself."

Liam leaned forward again. "Are you reporting directly to anyone about this case?"

"Why do you care?"

"Just answer."

Webb shrugged. "Nobody out of the ordinary. Just the sheriff."

"Is McBrien still the sheriff?"

Webb nodded. "How do you know that?"

"It's not my first time in this room, remember?"

"Yeah, I report to the sheriff—so what?"

"Has anybody else taken an unusual interest in the case? Asked questions about it? Followed very closely? Maybe offered to help?"

"This is a small place, Goetz. We don't get many murders, so, yeah, a lot of people in the office have been interested. Everybody has. Look," he continued, "I don't know what kind of game you're playing, but it's not going to work."

The man was confused, Liam knew, and irritated. Liam didn't blame him for either feeling. But Liam was pretty sure that whoever was behind the trafficking ring was going to burst in here at any minute. They would be carefully monitoring who Webb brought in. If they were paranoid—and they would be—they would look further than the cursory glance Webb had given Liam's record.

Whether Liam was in town because of the human-trafficking ring or not, whoever was behind it would not want an active Omega Sector agent talking to the person they were using as their puppet.

"Anything about the video strike you as odd, Webb? A burglar leaving her long brown hair—an easily identifying feature—down for everyone to see? The fact that the burglar didn't turn and run when she could've easily made it to the door?"

He had Webb's full attention now. But Liam was running out of time and he knew it.

"Something's not right. I think you know that," Liam whispered, leaning closer. "Don't let it go."

"Who are you?" Webb asked just as softly.

The door to the interview room opened and an older man walked in.

"Goetz, it's been quite a long time," the man said. "Didn't expect to see you here again."

Sheriff McBrien. Was he the one behind all this? Did he know that Liam was law enforcement?

Webb looked surprised to see his boss. "Wasn't expecting you this morning, Sheriff."

"Well, when I heard my old friend Goetz was

here, I thought I would stop by. What are you doing back around these parts?"

Liam still didn't know what McBrien knew, so he kept to his original story.

"I'm here visiting a friend."

"Vanessa Epperson?" McBrien asked.

"Yeah, we've sort of reconnected." Liam forced himself to relax in his chair. "You know, old flames and all that."

"It's been quite a long time, hasn't it?" McBrien cocked his head to the side. "Any particular reason why the flame has rekindled now?"

Liam shrugged with practiced nonchalance. "She called me out of the blue. Women. Hell if I understand them."

"I brought in Mr. Goetz to corroborate Ms. Epperson's story about her contact with the teenage runaway who may be our murder suspect." Webb was obviously trying to impress his boss with his thoroughness.

"And did you find out anything interesting?" Sheriff McBrien asked, coming to stand behind the seat next to Webb but not sitting.

Webb stared at Liam, but Liam didn't try to communicate anything. McBrien was too close, and too astute, for that. Liam willed the younger man to make the right decision and not say anything to McBrien about their hushed conversation a few moments ago.

"No, nothing particularly interesting," Webb muttered after a moment.

Liam forced himself not to breathe a sigh of relief.

"Mostly, I brought him in because of his past record," Webb continued.

The sheriff's eyes narrowed slightly. "Did Mr. Goetz say anything about his current occupation?"

Liam sat straighter in his seat.

Damn.

McBrien knew. *McBrien* was the one who had checked deeper into his record. And here he was, early on a weekend morning, checking on the situation personally rather than reading the report later.

Webb wasn't behind the trafficking ring. McBrien was.

"I probably shouldn't call you 'mister,' right, Goetz?" McBrien said, watching him closely. "You probably prefer the title 'agent,' since you work for Omega Sector."

"What?" Webb fairly spewed. "That wasn't in his record."

"Yeah, you have to dig a little deeper to find it. But it's there," McBrien said.

Liam met Webb's eyes.

That, he tried to communicate to the other man. *That is an example of what I meant when I asked about things that bothered you around here.*

All he could do was hope Webb would see it for himself.

Liam shrugged. "I'm not here on any official business. So, no, I didn't mention it."

"Were you going to keep letting Webb treat you like a suspect? How long were you planning to keep the fact that you're law enforcement from him?"

Liam knew he had to tread carefully. He didn't have a good reason to keep his occupation a secret from Webb. Under normal circumstances he would've made it known immediately. Professional courtesy.

"Like I said, my reason for being here was completely nonprofessional." Liam winked at them. "I think that Officer Atwood who came to the hotel on Tuesday can attest to that."

McBrien didn't look convinced.

"Look, I haven't really mentioned to Vanessa that I'm law enforcement. I don't know how that's going to go over, so I'd like to keep it quiet from her and tried to keep it quiet from your assistant sheriff here." Liam shifted his weight in his chair. "Webb was questioning me about that teenage kid. I don't know anything, just like Vanessa didn't know anything. I just thought I would keep my Omega tie out of it. Easier for everyone."

He turned to Webb. "Besides, sometimes mentioning you're a federal agent makes some people nervous. Not that Webb here had anything to be nervous about. He was just doing his job. A routine follow-up with me, given my tie with Vanessa."

McBrien looked over at Webb. "Is that right?"

"Yes, sir."

Liam smiled. "See? No harm, no foul. But if you don't mind, I'd like to wrap this up. I've got a place a hell of a lot more interesting to be than this room." He winked at the two men. "I'll be staying at Vanessa Epperson's apartment if you need me. That's where Webb picked me up."

Liam stood. He'd done all he could do. He just hoped McBrien bought it.

"Well, I apologize for my mistake," Webb said. "I hope there are no hard feelings."

Liam stuck his hand out to shake the younger man's. "You were just doing your job." He squeezed Webb's hand just slightly. "I hope you'll keep doing your job."

Get the message, kid.

Webb nodded. Liam hoped he understood.

McBrien was largely silent during the exchange. Liam wasn't able to read him. Was he suspicious?

As they exited the room McBrien slapped Liam on the back. "Well, I may not be sure exactly what happened here this morning, but I am very glad to see you found yourself on the right side of the law. Happy to have you as one of the good guys, Goetz."

He stuck his hand out. Liam forced himself to

shake it, although all he really wanted to do was to crush the man up against the wall and force him to tell where the girls were being held.

Liam had no doubt McBrien was behind this. He wanted to knock the smug look out of the other man's eyes and beat him until he fell to the floor.

"It's good to be one of the good guys, McBrien," he said instead.

Liam forced himself not to say anything further. Nothing sarcastic. Nothing that would give McBrien a hint that they were on to him. They walked the few steps to the lobby. Vanessa was there on the opposite side, looking in the other direction. She wasn't supposed to be here, but he was damn sure glad she was. Her presence gave added credibility to his lover story.

"But to be honest, I couldn't care less about good guys or bad guys," Liam murmured to the other men, gesturing to and all but leering at Vanessa. "I just care about *that*."

McBrien smirked. Webb pursed his lips in disapproval. Good, hopefully Liam wasn't wrong about the younger man and Webb would start really looking at what was going on around him. Liam had done all he could do to suggest there was a problem.

He knew both men were watching as he left them in the hallway and walked over to Vanessa. She was startled when she saw him, and stopped her worried shifting of her weight back and forth on her feet.

"I know I'm not supposed to be here—"

Liam kissed her.

He kissed her to stop her from accidentally saying anything that might go against his story. He kissed her to seal the story that he and Vanessa were lovers. He kissed her because...hell, for his entire life he'd never been in the same room as Vanessa and not wanted to kiss her.

But mostly he'd kissed her because he hadn't been able to this morning, after her news about all she'd lost—all they'd lost—eight years ago. He couldn't change the past, and didn't know what the future held, but right now he could kiss her.

He broke off the kiss a moment before it would've become uncomfortable for everyone.

"Thanks for coming to check on me," he said, leaning his forehead against hers. "I'm free to go."

But would he ever be free to leave Vanessa again? Liam had no idea.

Chapter Eighteen

"You weren't supposed to be here," Liam murmured to her as they walked across the parking lot together.

"I made Joe bring me," she said. "I wasn't sure what they were going to accuse you of, and I didn't want to leave you at Webb's mercy."

They made it to the car. Liam greeted Joe and they both got in the back. "Webb is not our guy."

"Really?" Vanessa stared at him. "What about all his questions and having a video clip that can't possibly be Karine?"

"I think he's being used to do someone else's dirty work. Webb's beginning to realize it, too."

"If the assistant sheriff isn't your guy, who do you think is?" Joe asked from the front seat.

Liam looked over at Vanessa. "Sheriff McBrien."

The sheriff. Vanessa could feel herself blanch. She and Liam had known the man most of their lives, although for Liam, not in a good way.

"*What?* Are you sure?" she asked.

"Webb may be a jerk with a political agenda, but he's not the one behind this. Webb can tell something is off about this entire investigation. He doesn't know what it is, but he knows something's not right."

"But *McBrien*?"

Marcus McBrien was an elected official, for heaven's sake. Knowing that someone you'd known for years was capable of such crimes against girls was sickening on multiple levels. To think about how long it could've been going on, right under everyone's noses…?

Almost unbearable.

"I started thinking it wasn't Webb as soon as he brought me in for questioning and didn't know I was Omega. It wouldn't take much extra work to get that information. Someone who has something to hide—especially something as big as a trafficking ring with a missing girl—would check me out more thoroughly."

"And the sheriff was that person," Joe confirmed for him.

"Yep. And McBrien was determined not to leave Webb alone with me once he figured out I was Omega."

Vanessa didn't necessarily consider herself a violent person, but if McBrien was here right now she would pound him into the ground with a baseball bat. And wouldn't lose a moment's sleep over it.

After she found out where he was keeping the girls, of course.

"You certain?" Joe asked from the driver's seat. "Should we pull Derek off tailing Webb and put him on McBrien?"

"Yeah." Liam nodded. "Webb isn't our guy. I may never be besties with him, but he's just trying to do his job."

Joe snickered at *bestie* and took out his phone to text. "I'll let Derek know, then take you guys back to Vanessa's place." He made eye contact with Vanessa through the rearview mirror. "That good?"

Vanessa smiled. "Yeah."

"She wasn't supposed to be here at all," Liam told Joe. "Good job on that."

"Hey." Joe started the car then held both hands up. "Don't look at me. She was coming here with or without me. Unless you wanted me to sit on her, the best I could do was tag along."

"Couldn't you use your super powers?" Liam asked. "I don't think sitting on her would be necessary."

Vanessa imagined no red-blooded woman would consider having someone with the charm and good looks of Joe sitting on her a bad thing, although she didn't mention that to Liam.

"Super powers?" she asked.

"Yeah." Liam smiled as Joe drove out of the sheriff's office parking lot. "Joe is a hostage negotiator for Omega. He can pretty much talk anybody into doing anything. It's his super power—charming the pants off everyone."

Vanessa had been so worried about Liam and what was happening at the sheriff's office that she hadn't paid much attention to Joe beyond a cursory appreciation of his good looks. Now she really studied him.

"Normally, I just try to charm the pants off women," Joe muttered. "Guys, I prefer, leave their clothes on."

"Oh, my gosh, you're Joe *Matarazzo*." Realization dawned and she saw him wince in the rearview mirror at the recognition. "I think our families were both in Vail or Aspen a couple years at the same time. All the girls were gaga over you."

Of course, the Matarazzo family had made the Epperson family wealth look like chump change. They were wealthy with a capital *W*. Like, trace-their-family-back-to-the-*Mayflower* prestigious.

Joe was one of the Matarazzo sons and very much a playboy.

"So you work for Omega Sector?" she asked. She couldn't imagine anyone bearing the Matarazzo name would ever need a job.

"Yeah, I found a skill set I was good at or, as jackass over here calls it, my 'super powers.'"

Their eyes met again in the rearview mirror. "Not that it helped me keep you at your place."

Joe looked over at Liam. "And you better shut up. I've got some secrets on you I'm sure you don't want shared, speaking of pants being off."

Vanessa studied scenery out the window at that. She knew Liam had had a life since they'd last seen each other. She'd even had a couple of relationships of her own since he'd left, however briefly. But she did not want to think about Liam with other women. Evidently, a *number* of other women.

Especially when she should've been the only woman in his life all this time. Would have been if they could've put their pride aside and fought for their relationship.

She should've tried harder to track him down. He should've come back and at least demanded to talk to her face to face.

They both should've handled it all so much differently.

Vanessa had never been too much of a romantic. Now, after years of being a social worker, she was even less so.

Eight years was a long time. The attraction was very definitely still there, but that wasn't enough. She was glad he now knew about the miscarriage, about what her parents had done—albeit to try to protect her—but ultimately that didn't change anything.

Vanessa looked at her hand that was linked with Liam's on his knee. They hadn't been able to figure out how to fight for their relationship when they were young and stupid and so in love with each other that it was tangible. How could they fight for it now when they were both so much more wary and wise?

And did they even want to fight for it?

Vanessa pushed all the questions out of her mind as they pulled up to her apartment complex. All that mattered right now was the safety of those girls. Whatever happened with Liam would happen. Vanessa wasn't going to worry about it now.

Joe—Joe *Matarazzo*, for heaven's sake— opened her door for her when they parked. It was still hard to believe the infamous playboy was now in law enforcement. He was one guy who would never be able to work undercover.

"I was just kidding about Liam with my comment," Joe said softly. "Just talking trash like team members do."

"Thanks." She raised an eyebrow at him. "But I think we both know there was quite a bit of truth to that jest."

"Just give him a chance," Joe said, his volume trailing off as they walked to the front of the car near Liam.

She glanced at both men. "The most important thing right now is to find those girls."

Joe nodded. "I'm heading back to Derek at the

sheriff's office. If we need to follow McBrien, it will have to be a two-car job."

Liam nodded. "I'll use the laptop to see if any of McBrien's known associates sets off any alarms in the Omega system. I'm sure he probably keeps himself pretty clean, though."

"Derek and I will do the same from the car."

"We're going to need to move fast if we get any information. I'm not sure if McBrien bought my excuse for being here, although I think he did."

"What excuse was that?" she asked.

Liam turned fully toward her. "You."

Oh.

With Liam looking at her that way, every thought she'd just had about their relationship not working out vanished. With just one look she was completely enthralled with him again. She forced herself to look away.

Focus on the girls.

"We're ready for either a water or a land siege." Joe's words interrupted her thoughts. "We can get a full SWAT team in from Norfolk if you want, but I doubt there's any way McBrien wouldn't hear about that."

"And immediately kill all the girls," Liam finished for him. "No, we're going to have to handle this on our own."

Joe nodded. "That's how I prefer it anyway."

Vanessa looked back and forth between the two

men. "You mean you guys are going to go onto the boat to get the girls?"

Liam cocked his head to the side and gave her that cocky smile she both loved and hated. "Hostage rescue. It's what I do, baby. Joe and Derek do the same thing, although Joe usually does a lot of talking with the perps beforehand."

Joe rolled his eyes. "It's not like I sit around and chat with them. But if there's any way of getting hostages out without using force in most situations, I try that. But not in this case. If we can get these girls out without being harmed, I don't give a damn whether those bastards are hurt in the process or not."

Liam looked at Vanessa. "If we can find out where the boat is, we can take it by stealth, or by more brutal means if necessary, as long as the girls won't be harmed. Or if they've moved to land, we're equipped for that, too."

Liam could handle himself. Even when they were younger, he'd had an awareness, a mental toughness that had gone way beyond someone of his teenage years. It had been one of the things that had drawn her to him.

But she still didn't like the thought of him risking his life. No amount of mental toughness could stop a bullet. The risks here were very real.

Liam took her hand. "Let's get some rest. You need a chance to regroup."

Vanessa nodded. Between talking about the

miscarriage, Liam being taken in for questioning and thinking about the danger he'd be in trying to get the girls out, she felt as if her world was flying apart in a hundred different directions.

"Keep us posted," he told Joe as the man got back into his car.

LIAM CHECKED HER apartment again before he would let her inside. The thought of eating crossed her mind, but she pushed it away. She just wanted to sleep. She barely remembered making it to her bed and falling on it. But when she woke up the sun was much lower in the sky and she could smell...bacon?

Her shoes were off and she'd been covered up, obviously by Liam. She made her way out of bed and into the kitchen. She found Liam there making breakfast food with ease.

"You cook?" The Liam she had known years ago couldn't boil water. He'd never had to worry about cooking with his grandmother around. Vanessa made her way over to the table and sat.

He turned and smiled. "I do all right with breakfast."

"Breakfast is your specialty, huh?" She tried to keep her tone light but could tell it fell short. Joe's insinuation about Liam's sexual exploits came back to mind.

Liam looked over at her, jaw set. "I won't lie

to you. There have been women since I left the Outer Banks."

"How many?" The words were out of her mouth before she could stop them. "Never mind. I really don't want to know."

She began playing with the napkin on the table. Did she want to know? No. She didn't want to think about Liam with one other woman, much less countless others. "I'm sure you've had other boyfriends."

"A couple, but never anything serious. And not for a pretty long while."

Liam didn't say anything, just finished cooking. He then put the bacon, eggs and toast on plates and carried them over to where she sat. He didn't sit himself.

"There were a lot," he admitted finally. "A lot of women over a lot of years."

Vanessa couldn't make eye contact with him anymore. She felt stupid for asking. She hadn't expected him to be true to a relationship that didn't exist. It had never even occurred to her.

But to hear that she had meant so little to him that there had been *a lot* of women? She felt daggers flying into her heart. "I understand," she finally said, her food untouched. "You had freedom, had opportunity, had a chance to make up for time you'd lost just being with me for so many years."

He just stood in front of her for a long moment, then put both hands on the back of her chair, trapping her there as he leaned down so their faces were closer together.

"You know, I told myself those very words for years. *Years*." His face inched closer. "And even more, I believed it. I believed that those women made me happy. Complete. A fun guy. That my freedom was the most important thing, and as long as I had that, I was golden. Had dodged a bullet by getting away from you. From us."

She couldn't breathe. She didn't want to hear this.

Liam dipped his head even lower so they were eye to eye. "It took me a long time to realize—"

His words were cut off by his phone ringing where it sat on the table.

"Damn it," he muttered. "It's Joe. I've got to take this."

He brought the phone to his ear. "Joe, this damn well better be the most important thing you've ever said."

Vanessa was close enough to hear Joe's response even though the phone was at Liam's ear.

Sheriff McBrien had somehow gotten away.

Chapter Nineteen

The conversation with Vanessa, as much as it needed to happen, would have to wait.

"Did you get made?" Liam asked Joe.

"No," Derek said, also on the line. "McBrien tricked us from the beginning. He sent someone out to his car around four o'clock. The guy had the same general build and coloring, so from our distance we thought it was him."

"Dude led us to a restaurant clear on the other side of the island," Joe continued. "We couldn't see inside, but we had both exits covered. When he came out an hour later, we realized we'd been set up."

Frustration knotted Liam's gut. He hadn't fooled McBrien this morning; the man was on to them.

"By the time we got back to the station, he had already left for real," Derek finished.

Liam walked out of the kitchen. He didn't want to have this conversation in front of Vanessa, although he knew there was really no help for that. No matter where he went in this tiny apartment, she'd still be able to hear him.

"Those girls are as good as dead," Liam mumbled. "McBrien is probably on his way out there right now to get rid of any evidence."

"Maybe not," Derek said. "He'll only do that as a very last resort because of all the money he stands to lose. Especially now that he's going to have to lie low for a while. If there's any way he can keep them alive, he'll try to."

Liam prayed that was true. But even if it was, it wouldn't matter. Unless they could pick up McBrien's trail again, they were no closer to knowing where the girls were than they had been days before.

"We're going to head back to you, formulate a plan," Joe said. "Maybe you should have Andrea try talking to Karine again. See if, now that a couple of days have gone by, she remembers anything."

"It's worth a shot. I'll call her. See you guys in a few minutes." He disconnected the call and turned to find Vanessa standing just a few feet behind him at the entrance of the living room, face pale.

"You heard?" he asked.

"I got the general gist. McBrien got away. Those girls are in even more trouble than before and we're back to square one."

Liam didn't even know how to soften that.

"Yeah. Basically. But I have been running Mc-Brien's known associates. Hopefully that will provide us with some info."

"What sort of people are you looking for?"

Liam shrugged a shoulder. "No any one characteristic in particular, but anything that might ring any bells. Maybe an old high school buddy he's known a long time and trusts implicitly. Or maybe a contact he's made more recently who might dabble in some illegal stuff on the side."

"It doesn't sound like something a computer can sort through."

"Definitely not. The Omega system can throw us info on people who have a criminal record, but McBrien won't have a lot. He's spent too many years keeping himself clean."

"So you're going through all this yourself."

Liam shrugged. "Me, the guys and Andrea. It's our best chance right now."

Liam knew it was a slim chance at best. Andrea was a hugely gifted profiler, even for her young age, but she couldn't pull something out of nothing. She would look for possible suspicious patterns with McBrien's associates—just as he, Joe and Derek would—but it was a time-consuming process and didn't guarantee results. If no one had ever seen McBrien with the men he was working with, there would be no possible link to them.

They could arrest McBrien, but it would be messy. No judge would allow them to hold him for long, and their only recourse would be to bring in Karine. Then it would be her word against the sheriff's. Traumatic for Karine and still wouldn't save the other girls.

If the worst possible scenario played out and they couldn't get the girls out safely, Liam would do his best to make sure McBrien went down for what he'd done to Karine at the very least. He would make sure the girl's story was told and her suffering wasn't in vain.

There was a knock on the door. Liam encouraged Vanessa to eat her food while he answered it, knowing it was Derek and Joe.

It wasn't. It was Assistant Sheriff Webb.

"You back to arrest me?" Liam asked.

"You should've told me from the very beginning you were Omega and almost all the questions could've been avoided," Webb replied.

Liam cocked one eyebrow. "You looking for an apology? Fine. Sorry I didn't tell you I was federal law enforcement."

Liam began to shut the door; he didn't have time to cater to the younger man's ego. Webb stopped him.

"No, I didn't come here for an apology. I came to tell you that you were right."

Those weren't the words Liam had been expecting.

Derek and Joe showed up behind Webb, both with their hands very close to their weapons.

"Guys, this is Assistant Sheriff Tommy Webb." He pointed to Derek and Joe. "Webb, these are my colleagues Agents Joe Matarazzo and Derek Waterman."

Webb nodded. "I guess you're not all here to see Vanessa Epperson. That seems to be the excuse de jour."

"No, we're not," Joe said. "But the real question is why are *you* here?"

"Let's at least get out of the hallway to have this conversation," Liam said, opening the door so everyone could enter. They all walked into the living room.

Vanessa joined them, coming to stand by Liam. "Why is he here?" she asked.

"We were just asking him ourselves."

The younger man was uncomfortable, Liam could tell. He didn't blame Webb. There was a lot of animosity in the room and it was mostly pointed at him.

"You guys want to tell me exactly what the hell is going on?" Webb's frustration and confusion were evident.

"Why don't you tell us what you know and we'll work from there?" Liam said.

"Well, I know for sure that you're not in town to canoodle with Vanessa." He looked closer to where Liam's arm had wrapped around her waist and pulled her next to him. "Or not *just* to canoodle."

"Canoodle?" One of Joe's eyebrows popped up.

"Whatever. I know that's not why he's here. You're all not here for some sort of romantic venture."

"Okay, brilliant detective work, Webb," Derek interjected. "What else do you know?"

"I know there's something going on in the department. It involves Sheriff McBrien and Dwayne Anderson, the AV guy for the crime lab."

Finally a name. Liam looked over at Derek.

"I'm on it. Computer in the kitchen?"

"Yeah." Derek would run Anderson and they would know anything there was to know about him within the hour. Hopefully it would be useful.

Webb watched Derek leave then turned back to Liam and the others. "I know it has something to do with that teenage runaway. The one accused of burglary and murder."

"Go on," Liam prompted.

"Well, I'd never heard anything about this girl at all, and then suddenly a week ago McBrien is asking me to personally find her. At first I didn't think anything of it. The sheriff's position is just as much political as it is law enforcement, so I thought maybe he was helping out a high-influence friend and trying to keep the situation under wraps. I honestly didn't think anything would come of it." He turned and pointed at Vanessa. "Until you showed up with her at the hospital.

"And then it got weird," Webb continued. "Girl wasn't at the hospital and McBrien got pretty stressed out when I told him she'd definitely been there but had run."

Webb began to pace.

"The next thing I know, we're doing car-to-car searches for some fugitive. We have a name but no real picture. The sheriff himself was searching cars. I've never seen that happen. Plus, he asks us to keep an eye out for the missing teenager while we're searching. Then the fugitive search stops as suddenly as it starts."

"Next thing I know, the teenage runaway we were searching for *discreetly* is a murder suspect and I'm supposed to question and perhaps even charge Vanessa Epperson for accessory."

Liam let him keep talking. It was important that Webb really understand for himself what was going on.

"So all the pressure to get this girl… Then, when I think I'm doing a good thing by bringing you in—" Webb turned to Liam "—the next thing I know, McBrien is letting you out. Just like you said he would. Because you're not only law enforcement, you're *elite* law enforcement. But McBrien never even asked you one thing about the case or the girl. He should've asked you, regardless if you were Omega Sector or not."

Liam nodded. "He was trying not to draw attention back to the girl. In case I really was here for Vanessa and not on official Omega business. McBrien wasn't sure which."

Webb nodded. "When the sheriff left this afternoon, I went into his office. It's not unheard of. I've done it before. The fact that he lets others in there is either really gutsy or means he doesn't leave anything incriminating in there and is trying to give the appearance of an open-door policy."

Liam shrugged. "McBrien is definitely smart. I'd doubt he'd leave anything lying around his office."

"Yeah. Well, he came *back* into his office after he left. I ducked into his private bathroom, but was just about to announce myself when he got a phone call. Something weird."

Liam took a step closer. "Do you remember what was said?"

"I don't have to remember. I already had my phone out to take pictures if I found anything. So I recorded it."

Webb took his phone out. He'd made a video recording of the conversation. The video only showed the back of the bathroom door, but the audio was clear, at least McBrien's side of it.

"Why are you calling me now, Anderson? I'm still at the office… Things are getting too complicated. We probably just need to get rid of the property and take the loss… Because there are people a lot smarter than Webb now involved. We just need to cut our losses… Fine, I'm listening. You have twenty seconds…

"Well, they certainly don't feel bad about taking advantage of our misfortune...I agree. Half is better than nothing. But it has to be tonight. If not, I'm going to get rid of it all personally... Okay, midnight, tonight. Harper's Cove. Don't call me again when you know I'm still at work."

Liam looked over at Joe. Midnight tonight at Harper's Cove. Liam knew where it was and knew it would be empty at this time of year.

The perfect place to sell the girls to some unknown buyer.

"So that's everything I have. You want to tell me what's going on?" Webb said.

Liam was willing to bet that Webb was a lot smarter than McBrien gave him credit for.

"Why don't you give me your best guess?" he said to the younger man.

"This missing teenager obviously has something on the sheriff. He was trying to find her quietly, through me and the bogus fugitive search. Then when that failed, he and Anderson killed some poor woman in her home and created some sort of phony murder video trying to frame or discredit the girl in case she came forward."

McBrien had definitely underestimated Tommy Webb.

"Human-trafficking ring," Liam told Webb. "One teenager—Karine—got away. There are seven more still on a boat somewhere."

Webb's curse was vile.

"We all agree with you," Vanessa said. "Liam

and I have known the sheriff nearly two decades. It's inconceivable that he's capable of something like that."

Webb cursed again.

"Do you still have the girl? Is she somewhere safe?" he asked after a moment.

"Yes, she's with another Omega agent, someone not associated with either Vanessa or me," Liam told him. "Safe."

"It's already six o'clock," Joe said. "We don't have long to plan this rescue attempt. We'll need to be in position before their boat arrives in the cove. They won't be expecting anyone to already be out there."

"If you attack the boat, McBrien will kill those girls. I'm sure of it," Webb said.

Joe shook his head. "We're not going to use force unless there's no other option. Our plan is stealth. With any luck, we'll get the girls out before we even confront McBrien and whoever is with him."

"And by *confront*, Joe means take that son of a bitch down," Liam said. "I can guarantee that."

Chapter Twenty

Liam, Joe and Derek had done this before. It didn't take more than five minutes of hearing them plan for that fact to become obvious to Vanessa. They trusted each other. They respected each other.

They planned to get those girls out or to die trying.

Webb had helped them move an impressive amount of equipment, all in large black boxes, from Joe's and Derek's cars into her apartment. Then Webb left. He had his own role to play in this mission. He wouldn't be going out to the boat, but he would be making sure the buyers didn't escape after Liam and the guys got the girls out.

Vanessa just tried to stay out of the way as the men unpacked the boxes with certain things she recognized—guns, knives, some sort of dive skins—and many things she didn't. As they sorted and repacked what they would need, they discussed different possible scenarios.

"You're talking about a half dozen traumatized teenagers. They might try to fight us," Joe pointed out.

"Try to mention Karine's name if you can," Liam responded as he took a large duffel bag out of one of the boxes. "But we'll have to subdue them if necessary."

Vanessa hoped that wouldn't be necessary. She was sure the girls had been traumatized enough already.

They would be using some sort of watercraft they called a Zodiac, which was quiet and easy to maneuver. It was black and had no lights or reflective material on it, they explained. They would use an underwater trolling motor as long as they could then guide it the rest of the way manually.

The men themselves would also be in all black, using the cover of night to provide them with the stealth they needed to pull this off. A storm was brewing overhead. That would work to their advantage in masking sound.

Liam's background in Special Forces was obvious in everything he did as he situated himself for the operation. His placement of weapons, his ease with all the equipment, even the way he carried himself now that he was in full agent mode bespoke it.

"I wish there was something I could do," she said to him as the guys finished up with their final preparations. "Staying at the house with Karine doesn't seem like a very helpful position. What if we waited on the dock by the cove? That way when you guys got off the water she would be right there to reassure the girls."

Liam reached over and tucked a strand of her hair behind her ear, then cupped the back of her head with his large hand. "No. It leaves you too much out in the open. Knowing you're safe is the only way I can do this. It allows me to totally focus on those girls and getting them out. Besides, Andrea will be at the dock. Her presence will help the girls."

Andrea and Karine were on their way now to pick Vanessa up. Liam didn't want to take any chances on Vanessa being followed and Andrea would be able to spot and hopefully lose anyone tailing them.

"I don't like that you're the one taking all the chances."

"Risks are part of my job, but I've trained for them. Joe and Derek, too. This is what we do."

She hooked her hand around his arm, causing his elbow to bend and bring his face closer. "You just be careful."

"I will."

"And call me as soon as you've got them so I can bring Karine to see them."

"Yes, ma'am." Liam gave her a crooked smile and she felt her stomach do a little somersault.

She felt her phone buzz. Andrea was here to get

her. It was just as well; Vanessa couldn't watch them prep any more. Every weapon she saw just reminded her of how much danger they would be in.

The sun was going down. They would be leaving soon. She said her goodbyes to Joe and Derek, and Liam walked her out to her car. He greeted Andrea and Karine.

"Tonight," he told Karine. "We're going to get the other girls out tonight. We know where they're going to be."

"Good," Karine said. "Thank you, Mr. Liam."

"Andrea will bring you as soon as we have them. We will probably need to meet at the hospital. That's the best place for them to go."

Karine flinched but nodded.

"It will be safe for them there. I promise."

"Okay."

Liam smiled at her. "Right now you and Vanessa are going to stay at the house. I'll call her first thing when you can see them."

He turned to Vanessa and opened the back door to the car for her. "Text me when you're at the house so I know you're okay."

She reached up and grabbed the center of his tight black shirt, pulling him closer. "Be. Careful."

She knew she had already said it, but she couldn't stop herself from saying it again.

"I will. Promise. This time tomorrow we'll be finishing up the conversation from the kitchen."

The one where he'd admitted to having been involved with *a lot* of women? She wasn't sure she wanted that. But she was willing to discuss darn near anything with him if it meant he was back safely.

"Deal," she whispered.

He kissed her softly. Sweetly.

Vanessa forced herself to step back. She had to leave now or she was never going to. She smiled at him and got in the car.

It was good that Andrea was driving, watching for anyone who might be following, because Vanessa was pretty much useless. Someone could've been directly behind them, high beams blazing, and Vanessa probably wouldn't have noticed. She was too busy thinking about Liam.

She just wanted this to be over. Wanted those girls to be safe. Wanted him and his friends to be safe, also.

Vanessa forced herself to focus. Liam and the team seemed more than prepared. They had all the equipment—under-water, above-water—they needed. When he had been in the army and she had waited at home, she'd never doubted his abilities. She wasn't going to start doubting them now.

The trip to the house Andrea had rented was made in silence, everyone focused on their own thoughts. It wasn't long before they pulled up there.

"You gals wait here while I secure the building," Andrea told them, leaving the car running. She took out her weapon—just as Liam had done every time they'd entered her apartment—and disappeared inside.

She was back in just over a minute.

"All clear," she said then smiled at Vanessa. "There's no reason to think this place has been compromised, and there definitely wasn't anybody tailing us, but precaution."

Vanessa smiled back. "I understand." She wasn't willing to take any chances with Karine's safety, either.

Andrea walked Vanessa and Karine in the front door. The two women had obviously made themselves comfortable here. Karine immediately kicked off her shoes and headed straight for the fridge.

"I've basically been allowing her to eat whatever she wants, whenever she wants," Andrea whispered. "I figured, after everything, there couldn't be any real harm in that."

"Absolutely agree. Gallons of ice cream can probably help soothe any trauma. Or at least much more so than vegetables."

"She's been doing pretty well. Has woken up crying a few times and spends a lot of her time looking out at the water. But she's keeping it together. She's strong."

Vanessa nodded and watched Karine plop down on the couch, yogurt in hand—at least it wasn't ice cream—and turn on the television. "She's amazing."

"She'll have to heal on her own timetable. Nobody can set that for her," Andrea said, and then walked into the kitchen herself.

Sounded as though Andrea knew that from experience. She'd like to get to know the other woman better, but now wasn't the time.

"Okay, I'm going to meet Webb and help coordinate the Coast Guard's efforts." Andrea grabbed a water bottle from the fridge. "We want to catch McBrien and his buddies, but we also want the buyers, too. You guys stay here and wait for our call."

"How long do you think it will be?" Vanessa asked.

"It's hard to say. These types of ops have a lot of factors, and any one of them can affect the timetable. I would tell you to go to sleep, but I know you won't. But it will be after midnight, probably, before Karine will be able to see the girls."

If we can get the girls out alive. Andrea's eyes said it and Vanessa was glad she didn't say the actual words.

"After the call, someone will come get you to take you to them, okay?"

Vanessa watched as Andrea made her way over to Karine. She hugged the girl and whispered something to her. Karine nodded then sat back down.

"Follow behind me and lock the door," Andrea told Vanessa. "I know it doesn't have to be said, but don't decide to go for a walk or swim or anything. Just stay inside until we come for you."

Vanessa rolled her eyes. "Yeah, no worries. We'll binge watch some sitcoms or something if we can't sleep."

She knew she wouldn't sleep a wink. Not until she knew the girls were free and Liam was okay.

She locked and bolted the door behind Andrea then headed back into the living room. Karine was staring blankly ahead of her, yogurt still in her hand.

"You doing all right?" Vanessa asked as she sat slowly next to the girl on the couch.

"I hope everyone will be okay," Karine said.

"Liam is the very best, honey. His friends are, too. They'll get the girls out."

Karine nodded and scooted closer to Vanessa. "Okay, good."

"You'll need to be ready to see them and reassure them in the hospital. Do you want to go to sleep? Get some rest while you can?"

"No," the girl whispered. "I cannot sleep. It is hard to sleep always, but tonight I know I cannot."

Vanessa understood. "Then we'll just watch TV, okay? If we fall asleep, that's fine. If not, that's okay, too. What do you want to watch?"

Vanessa changed into shorts and a T-shirt before they searched through the channels until they found reruns of *The Brady Bunch*. When the channel promised they'd be playing the show all night, Vanessa and Karine settled back on the couch.

Vanessa lost count of how many episodes they'd watched—six? seven?—when she was about to ask Karine if they should turn to something else. No matter what decade the show was viewed, Jan was still so annoying.

Vanessa shot off the couch when she heard a voice behind them.

"It's so good to see young people watching something wholesome like *The Brady Bunch* rather than the smut normally found on television."

It was Sheriff McBrien. And he had his gun pointing right at them.

Chapter Twenty-One

Karine immediately began crying and cowering behind Vanessa. Vanessa put an arm around the girl and kept her pressed up to her back.

"You here to arrest me again, Sheriff? A gun isn't really necessary."

"I think we both know we're way past arresting. That's not really going to work at all."

Vanessa forced herself to look the older man in the eye without flinching. "How did you find us?"

"Webb."

Vanessa blanched; she couldn't help it. "Webb's working with you?"

McBrien rolled his eyes. "No. I can barely stand having that goodie-goodie around at the office, much less during personal business."

Vanessa tightened her arm around Karine. She wouldn't let this man hurt her again.

"Evidently he overheard a call today. Would've gotten away with it, too, if I hadn't had to go back into my office five minutes after the first time. Secretary asked if I had run into Webb, since evidently he'd been in there the first time."

Vanessa didn't say anything. She didn't want to confirm any details for McBrien.

"He was hiding in my private bathroom, I think. Normally that would just slightly annoy me." He gestured toward Karine behind Vanessa. "But with missy here getting away, and your Omega Sector boyfriend showing up, I couldn't just assume Webb was ignorant of what was going on."

He took a step toward Vanessa and she took a step back with Karine.

"I should just kill you now, but I'm too greedy. I want the money I can get for her." McBrien's face took on an ugly hue. "Plus, I might be able to get a bonus for you. You're pretty old as far as these things go, but I'm sure our buyers could find a use for you."

Karine began silently sobbing behind her. Vanessa had to force herself not to retch. She would not give in to fear. "Liam will stop you."

"You mean Special Agent Goetz, who is on his way to Harper's Cove? Yeah, sorry to tell you, once I knew Webb had heard me, I changed the location of the meeting with the buyers. Goetz can check the cove all he wants. We won't be there."

Vanessa had to figure out a way to get a message to Liam, but McBrien was having none of that.

"I'll need your phone, Miss Epperson."

Vanessa backed away again, but McBrien rushed forward, grabbed her by her shirt and threw her to the floor. Then he grabbed Karine.

The girl began sobbing louder.

"Shut up. You're the root of all my problems." He raised a fist in front of Karine. "Your phone, Vanessa, or the buyers will get one girl with quite a few bruises. Although I'm sure they'll be all right with that."

Karine's face was ghostly pale.

"No, don't hurt her." Vanessa scrambled to her feet. "Here's my phone. Here."

She thrust it at him and rushed to Karine, grabbing her away from him. She put her arms around the girl, trying to protect her even though Karine was almost as tall as she was.

McBrien threw her phone to the floor and stomped on it. It broke into pieces. Useless.

How would she contact Liam now?

McBrien pulled out handcuffs, cuffed both of them with their arms behind their backs, and pulled them to the front door.

He got right in Vanessa's face. "I'm here in uniform with a patrol car. If you scream, I will tell people you're on drugs and then I will make the next few hours of your life as miserable as humanly possible." He pointed to Karine. "I will make hers even worse. Got it?"

Vanessa nodded.

"Quiet," he said to Karine, who nodded. He obviously didn't know how well Karine spoke English.

There was no one around for them to yell to on the walk to the car anyway; not that Vanessa would've risked it. McBrien had real nerve showing up in an official sheriff's vehicle as if he wasn't committing some of the most heinous crimes possible. But he was smart; it was the perfect cover.

If he could get Vanessa and Karine and the other girls to the buyers, they'd be gone forever and the only bit of evidence against McBrien would be a convoluted recording that didn't directly mention any crimes.

If he couldn't get Vanessa and Karine to the buyers, all he'd need to do was shoot them and say they'd come at him in a life-threatening manner and he had to defend himself. After all, there was already a recording of Karine killing someone else.

They were in trouble and Vanessa could not figure out how to get out of this. The only option she could see was to try to tackle McBrien herself while Karine ran. It wasn't a great plan. McBrien probably had six inches and seventy-five pounds on her, not to mention the added handicap of both her and Karine having their hands cuffed behind their backs.

But she knew if she let McBrien get them on whatever boat he was taking them to, she'd never be able to get Karine safely off again.

Vanessa didn't even let herself think about the

other girls. There was nothing she could do to help them now. All she could do was try to save Karine's life.

She felt the girl push closer to her where they sat in the back of the squad car and wished she could put her arm around her. Not that it would be much comfort in this situation.

Karine pushed up against her again and Vanessa looked over at her.

"I'm sorry, honey. I know you're scared," she whispered.

Karine pushed up against her again and whispered something, but Vanessa didn't know what.

"Just be ready to run when I make my move," Vanessa said in the lowest voice possible. "Run as fast as you can."

Vanessa doubted it would be enough. But it was their only option.

Karine shook her head and brushed up against her again.

"Hey, shut up back there," McBrien told them. "Or I can break your jaws and make you shut up."

Vanessa looked over at Karine. Hopefully the girl had heard her and understood the plan. Despite McBrien's threats, she seemed to be keeping it together, although she kept pressing against Vanessa.

Then Vanessa felt Karine's hand touch hers from behind them. She had to hold her arms at an awkward angle to make the contact, and Vanessa knew she must be terrified to want human contact enough to hurt herself for it.

She felt Karine press something into her hand. Karine wasn't looking for contact at all.

She was giving Vanessa her phone.

McBrien had assumed Karine didn't have one. Heck, Vanessa had even forgotten about it in the chaos.

There were only so many numbers programmed into the phone Liam had given the girl. Hers. Andrea's. Liam's. It was a cheap, prepaid flip phone and Vanessa wasn't entirely sure about the buttons. She felt out the number pad as carefully as she could with her fingers and then pressed what she thought was the 2 and Send.

She didn't know if they were the right buttons. She didn't know if it was even the right phone being called. She didn't know if Liam would even have his phone on, since he was in the middle of a mission where silence was important.

Those were a lot of ifs.

But it was their only chance.

SITTING IN THE middle of Harper's Cove, low in the Zodiac, everyone wearing night-vision goggles to see in case the boat with the girls also wasn't using any lights, Liam knew something was wrong.

"There should've been movement by now. From somewhere," he muttered.

There was no sign of the boat with the girls; no sign of the buyers. No sign of *anyone* out here.

"Even with the storm we've got pretty good visual, Liam," Derek said. "If there was someone out here, we'd be able to see them."

"Maybe something got changed. Time. Place," Joe said.

Maybe McBrien and his buddies had reconsidered and decided to just cut their losses and kill the girls.

Nobody said it, but all three men were thinking it.

Liam got out his phone. "I'm going to call Andrea. Maybe she's heard something from Webb."

Liam got his phone out of the waterproof casing attached to his specialized wet suit. As he reached to press Andrea's stored number, he was surprised when his phone buzzed in his hand.

Karine.

Why was she calling him?

He brought the phone to his ear. "Karine?"

Nothing.

"Karine?" he said again.

They were safe at the house. Maybe she butt-dialed him by accident, but Liam wasn't taking any chances.

Both Derek and Joe were watching him. "Call Vanessa," he told Joe. "I don't want to hang up here in case this is a problem."

He turned to Derek. "Get Andrea or Webb or someone to go to the house."

Both men were already ripping out their phones to make the calls.

"Karine?" Liam said again, keeping his voice quiet, since he wasn't sure of the situation. If this was just an accidental call, she would realize it soon.

But the fact that they were sitting in an empty cove, with no missing girls in sight, made Liam believe this was not just an accidental call. He kept his ear to the phone as the other men made their contacts. Derek was soon talking to Andrea, but Joe almost immediately had his phone back down.

"Vanessa's went straight to voice mail."

Damn it.

"I had a tracker app put on Karine's phone, just in case she went out somewhere and got lost." He gave Joe the information. "Find out where she is."

Joe started running the phone-finding app on his own device. Derek disconnected his call.

"Andrea is on her way to the house now. She should be there in less than ten minutes," Derek reported.

"Has she been able to contact Vanessa or Karine?"

"No. She's going to keep trying."

"I've got a ping on Karine's phone," Joe said. "She's not at the house, that's for sure."

Liam muttered a curse under his breath.

"They're in a moving vehicle heading toward the water," Joe said.

Derek started the engine on the Zodiac. Not the silent one, the big one. Built for speed.

"Which direction?" he asked.

"Looks like, based on your report, near that island where your car was pushed off the bridge."

"That's not too far from here by water," Liam said, pointing to the direction they needed to go. "It's around the inlet."

It was also an ideal place for some sort of shady deal to go down. There wouldn't be any car traffic at this time of year, and boats could get to it easily.

Liam muted his end of the phone so the noise wouldn't come through the other side, but kept his ear to it in case Karine or Vanessa said anything.

The situation had just gone from bad to nearly impossible.

Chapter Twenty-Two

Vanessa recognized their location as McBrien drove over the bridge. This was the place where she and Liam had almost died two nights ago. Although it was on the other side of Nags Head, by boat it wasn't all that far from where Liam and the team were.

If she could just let him know her location... She had no idea if the phone was even working.

McBrien parked the car and dragged them out of the backseat and toward a boat. Karine did her best to help hide the phone by walking as close behind Vanessa as possible.

The sheriff moved in front of them as they walked out to the small dock where the boat was tied off. Vanessa pressed the phone into Karine's hands.

"Put it in my pocket," she whispered. There was no way Vanessa could maneuver her arms to slide it into the front pocket of the loose shorts she was wearing.

"Shut up back there," McBrien barked.

"She's scared, McBrien. Just chill out."

The sheriff turned to glare at them. "She should be scared."

Let him glower. Karine had gotten the phone into Vanessa's pocket. It was still open and still running, as far as Vanessa knew. She had heard something at the beginning of the call that she was pretty sure was Liam, but there was only silence now. She was going to keep the call open in case that would help him.

McBrien dragged them onto the boat. The same one that held the girls. Vanessa looked at Karine. The girl's face held no color whatsoever. Vanessa couldn't imagine what a nightmare it must be for her to be coming back here.

As the boat pulled away, McBrien unlocked their handcuffs. "I don't think there is any need for those, but they can go right back on if there is any sort of problem."

Vanessa nodded and immediately put her arms around Karine. She wouldn't give McBrien any reason to use the cuffs again. If they jumped overboard—*when* they jumped overboard—it would be critical for their arms not to be locked behind their backs.

The girls were nowhere to be seen, probably still captive below. Vanessa saw two men besides

McBrien. One was driving the boat and the other made his way over to the sheriff.

"I thought you said you were going to kill them," the man said to McBrien.

Vanessa's arms tightened around Karine.

McBrien rolled his eyes. "Relax, Anderson, we can still get rid of them if we need to. But I thought it was better to see if we could get more money for them from the buyers. Especially since we're going to have to lie low on shipments for a while. The heat is too high. Going to be too high for a long time."

So this was Anderson, the guy Webb had mentioned. Karine refused to look at him, huddled into Vanessa. If Vanessa had a gun right now, she would probably kill all the men on this boat.

But she didn't have a gun; she only had her wits, a terrified teenager attached to her side and more traumatized girls in the hull of the boat.

She prayed Liam was on the open line of the phone in her pocket. She had to try to help him. Get McBrien talking so hopefully Liam would have a clue as to where they were.

"It must have made you pretty nervous when Liam and I were out here so close to the action the other night. Was it you who rammed the car off the bridge?" she ask the sheriff.

"No." He actually chuckled. "That was Anderson here. He didn't know who you were at the time, just knew you were snooping around where you didn't belong."

"What about Webb? He was out there, too. You didn't try to kill him."

Anderson finally spoke up. "Webb always checks out Riker's Island after he goes to Sally's diner on Thursday nights. He's nothing if not a creature of habit. We knew about Webb, expected him. We just didn't know about you. Were you following Webb or on to the location?"

"We were following Webb, actually. We thought he was behind this."

"See, Anderson, all that for naught." McBrien slapped the other man on his back. "I told you drowning them was overkill. They were after Webb the whole time. As if he is intelligent enough to get away with something like this."

"So he's not in on this with you?" Vanessa figured her best bet was still to play as dumb as possible. Not give away any clues about what they knew or didn't know, or where Liam was.

"Really, he didn't come blubbering to you in his normal Boy Scout way? I'm surprised. I would've thought he'd report back to you as soon as possible once he heard me on the phone."

"I don't know." Vanessa shrugged. "Liam was going into Norfolk to tell them his theory. Get backup or whatever. I haven't seen him or Webb since we were at the sheriff's office."

"Do you hear that, McBrien? This place is

going to be swarming with cops soon." Anderson was pacing, agitated.

McBrien frowned, narrowing his eyes. "They know nothing. Have nothing. Nobody can tie us to anything that has happened."

"But what about Webb? And her boyfriend, the Omega agent guy?"

"They can't prove anything. As long as you don't say anything or do anything stupid, we'll be fine. I've got measures in place to cover us."

Anderson looked ready to crack right now. Vanessa knew he'd never be able to hold up against Liam once questioning began. Liam would uncover the truth.

Vanessa and Karine might not be around to see it, but Liam would make sure these men paid for their crimes. That was comforting. Not much, but a little.

The boat slowed. They had to be close to where McBrien planned to meet the buyers.

"How did you find us at the house?" Vanessa asked him. In part to stall but also because she was interested.

"Once I figured out your boyfriend was an Omega agent, I figured there was no way he was here just to see you." McBrien shrugged. "No offense."

Vanessa didn't respond.

"I figured if this one—" he pointed at Karine "—was anywhere, it must be with you guys. It's off season, not a lot of rentals. Easy enough to find one rented by Andrea Gordon, who just happens to also be an Omega agent. It would be quite a co-incidence to have two Omega agents vacationing here on the same weekend."

"That Omega agent we were staying with just went out to get some groceries. She'll be back. Soon. And will be looking for us."

McBrien didn't look concerned. "I guess she'll wonder where you guys went."

"It will seem very suspicious."

"Not with the footage Anderson has concocted. We'll just add a little clip of you in there in the doctored footage of the burglary-murder. Then basically it will look like you waited for your chance and then you ran."

Vanessa had to admit, McBrien seemed to have thought everything through. His job as sheriff already gave him a platform from which to declare his innocence. Without Vanessa and Karine around to directly accuse him of anything, all evidence against him would be circumstantial at best.

"I see the buyers, boss." The big man behind the wheel spoke for the first time.

McBrien looked down at his watch. "Good. Right on time. Pull up. I'll bring them on here to look at the merchandise." He turned to Anderson. "You and Paul get the girls ready below. I'll keep these two with me.

He grabbed Vanessa with one arm and Karine

with the other, separating them. Vanessa struggled and McBrien backhanded her. She felt blood pool in her mouth.

McBrien smiled. "The buyers might like a little appetizer before the main meal."

"I'VE GOT TWO boats in my sight, Liam," Derek said.

Liam had hooked the phone to his ear via an earbud so he could hear what was going on at the other end over the motor of the Zodiac.

Vanessa and Karine were still alive. The relief Liam had felt at hearing Vanessa's voice had overwhelmed him. He couldn't hear her well, but he realized she was trying to give them clues as to where McBrien was holding them. She didn't realize he could track Karine's phone.

Damn McBrien. The man was smart. And he was right; without Vanessa and Karine's testimony, they didn't have very much on him. Even the call Liam was overhearing would probably prove worthless in court. There were too many factors distorting the sound. Any good lawyer would argue that what Liam thought he heard was actually something else.

But that didn't matter because Liam very much planned to have Vanessa and Karine alive and well to testify against McBrien.

Joe had slowed the Zodiac and was now using the quieter trolling motor. About a hundred yards from both boats, they stopped completely. This was as close as they could get without being heard, even with the choppy waves from the storm coming up. They were already pushing it.

They watched with their night-vision goggles as the two boats moved next to each other. Liam disconnected the call and took his earpiece out. He couldn't take the phone into the water with him, although he hated to lose the connection. Now was the time for action.

Rage boiled through him as he saw McBrien roughly separate Vanessa and Karine, then hit Vanessa in the face for some reason. She staggered but didn't fall.

Liam took a step toward them on the Zodiac, unable to help himself. "I'm going to kill that son of a bitch," he said.

"Keep focused, Liam," Derek muttered, having seen what happened. "If you don't, you won't be able to make the smart decisions. The decisions that are going to get everyone out of here safely."

"He just backhanded her." Liam could barely get the words out around his clenched jaw. "You have no idea—"

"I have no idea?" Derek cut him off. Even in the dark Liam could see the other man's raised eyebrow. Derek did know. He knew exactly what Liam was going through. Just six months ago a drug lord had held Derek's wife, Molly, at gunpoint and had hurt her without Derek being able to do anything about it. Had hurt her worse than just a backhand.

"I'm sorry. I just—" Liam bit off the words. "It's hard to not rush in there guns blazing."

Derek nodded. "I know. But we get Vanessa out just like we got Molly out. By being smart."

"Um, just want to remind you that Liam also drove a vehicle through Molly's front door. Not sure exactly how *smart* that was," Joe commented.

"Shut up, Joe." Liam's words held no sting. "We got the job done. That's what counts."

And they would get the job done now. Liam took a deep breath and pushed his rage deep down. He'd pull it back out if and when he needed it. "We infiltrate from the back. Get the girls out. Maybe seeing us pound on their captors might help them trust us a little. Once we've secured the area, gotten the girls in the water, I'm going to go up to the front. I'll handle that. Remember, quiet until there are no other options."

"Roger that," Joe responded.

The men readied themselves and their weapons, knowing this was the perfect time to move with the chaos of both boats coming together. It would be loud and rocky. And since their Zodiac was nearly impossible to detect in the darkness of the water—thank God for a moonless, stormy night—McBrien and his men would have no reason to be suspicious.

All three men entered the water with no sound

and swam quietly toward the rear of McBrien's boat. Liam and Joe silently treaded water, weapons raised, as Derek made it up the ladder. He then took out his weapon and covered Liam then Joe as they followed.

Liam could hear McBrien talking in the front of the boat. The thought of Vanessa there with him, with people who were here to buy and sell other humans, made him sick.

Derek communicated via hand signal that he was about to open the door leading to the galley. This was it. They had to get down there quietly and take out the two men before either of them could alert McBrien.

At the slightest crack of the door, they could hear girls crying. Joe's faced hardened as Liam gave him the nod to go forward. Liam followed, with Derek bringing up the rear, facing the back door so no one could sneak up on them.

The smell of unwashed flesh and human waste was overpowering as they moved farther into the galley. This hull was meant for two people for a couple days at most, not seven girls for nearly a week.

Joe rounded a corner—a tiny hall that housed probably a restroom and closet—and kept his weapon and eyes focused in front of him, giving a signal with his hand that what he could see was clear. In standard procedure, Liam moved past

Joe into the forward-most position. He took a few more steps up to the corner.

He brought his head around and then back in an instant.

The two men weren't paying any attention to the back of the room. They were too busy scoffing and gawking at the girls as they threw clothes at them and told them to change. The girls didn't understand and most were crying.

The youngest one—good Lord, she could only be eight or nine—was far in the back, obviously being protected by the other older girls. From where she sat on the floor, she could see Liam. She stared at him with big, dark eyes.

Liam gestured for her to be quiet, but had no idea if she knew what he meant. She just kept staring.

It was time for the attack. Every moment they wasted, they could lose the element of surprise. He felt Joe and Derek flank him. With hand signals he told them he would take the man furthest away and Joe was to take the one closest. Derek would continue to guard the door behind them.

This had to be quiet and fast. Anything else would probably cost Vanessa and Karine their lives.

On his count Liam and Joe flew around the corner. Both kidnappers had weapons they reached for but never even got close to getting them out.

From the corner of his eye Liam could see Joe

take down Anderson. A quick uppercut to the jaw, followed by a hard right, had the man dropping to the floor. A third hit to the face knocked Anderson completely out.

Liam's target was much bigger. Liam shot a modified karate chop to the guy's throat, in essence rendering him voiceless. With him unable to warn anyone, Liam completed the process of taking the perp out. He couldn't deny that every blow felt good. Even when the man was on the floor, Liam kept punching him. When he thought about what this guy had done to Karine, to these girls—

"Liam, enough, man." Joe's hand on his shoulder stopped him. Liam looked over, almost startled to see him there.

"He's out," Joe continued. "Let's get the girls off the boat."

Yes, that was the most important thing. Focus, Goetz. "Yeah, secure these two and let's get going."

He turned to face the girls, who were all staring at him with terrified eyes.

Chapter Twenty-Three

Watching him pound someone into the floor, even one of their captors, probably had not helped him establish any trust with the girls. But Liam couldn't do anything about that now.

"We help," he said slowly, softly. He wanted to use the shortest sentence possible, since he wasn't sure how much English anyone knew, if any.

None of them was crying or screaming, but none of them ran in his direction, either.

"Karine sent us."

He had their attention.

"Karine?" one of the oldest girls said. "She is alive?"

"Yes," Liam said, smiling as gently as he could. "But we need to get out of here now."

He waited while the girl explained what was going on in their native tongue.

"We must go. Swim to our boat," he told them.

"No, too far?" the same girl said. "Sharks. The man told us there were sharks."

They didn't have time for this, but the last thing Liam wanted was seven hysterical girls on his hands. They were barely holding it together as it was.

"What's your name?" Liam asked the older girl.

"Julia," she responded softly, the *j* sounding like a *hoo*.

"Julia, no sharks," Liam said. "I promise." He was telling the truth. There might be some out in the ocean, but there wouldn't be any in the bay.

Julia spoke to the other girls again. After a few seconds they nodded. All except for the little one, who began crying.

"What's wrong?" Liam asked.

"Liam, we've got to go. McBrien is going to be looking for these guys any minute," Derek said softly from the doorway.

Joe stood from tying and gagging the two men. "I'm ready. They're secure."

"Why is she crying?" Liam asked about the little girl.

"She doesn't know how swim."

Liam met Joe's eyes. "Can you carry the little one? Derek can lead the others. I have to get to Vanessa and Karine."

"No problem," Joe said, making his way toward the little girl.

She immediately jumped back and began sobbing.

"No, no. Shh," Joe said, backing up.

"Can you tell her he's going to carry her in the water, to the safe boat?" Liam asked Julia. "Joe is very strong and very kind. He will not let anything happen to her."

Julia crouched near the little girl and obviously tried to explain, but the girl just cried harder. She kept pointing to Liam.

Joe walked over to Liam, putting more distance between him and the little girl, since his nearness seemed to upset her.

"Liam, we're going to have to subdue her if she doesn't calm down," Joe said. "I hate to do that, but it might be the only way."

"I agree, Liam. We need to move. *Now,*" Derek chimed in.

"Julia, we've got to go. Make her understand."

"I'm sorry." Julia looked up at Liam from where she was crouched. "She only wants to go with you."

"Me?" That wasn't what he had been expecting.

"There's no accounting for women's taste, man. Just do it, Liam," Joe murmured. "Let's get out of here."

Liam reached down and scooped up the little

girl. She immediately stopped crying and put her arms around his neck.

"Okay, let's go." He led them up the stairs. The girls followed behind him, with Joe and Derek bringing up the rear.

Out of the bottom cabin they made it to the back of the boat. Liam immediately made his way down the ladder into the water, the little girl's arms still trustingly wrapped around his neck. He had no idea why she trusted him, but he was glad to get her out of that hell.

It occurred to Liam that had he and Vanessa's child lived, he or she would've been just about the age of this child now. Somewhere a mother and father were distraught about their missing daughter. Liam vowed he would see their family reunited.

He heard her gasp at the cold water, but she didn't cry or do anything else. The water was pretty chilly and the girl wasn't wearing much clothing.

"Okay, sweetie, I need you around on my back," he whispered once they were fully in the water. He knew she didn't understand, but when he shifted her weight around to his back, she went easily. He could still feel her little arms around his neck.

Liam glanced back to see that Derek and Joe were successfully getting the other girls into the water and began swimming when he saw that they were down. He swam fast, not waiting for the girls to keep up. He needed to get back to the boat to help Vanessa and Karine.

The girl held tightly to his neck, giving him free range of movement. It only took a few minutes to get her to the Zodiac. He tossed her light body over the side and she giggled just the slightest bit.

"You stay here. Okay?" He held his hand out in a stop gesture then pointed inside the Zodiac.

The girl nodded. Liam touched her cheek softly then was gone, swimming silently back toward McBrien's boat. He passed Joe and Derek on the way with the other girls.

"Get them to safety," he told Joe. The girls seemed to be doing okay, but all of them were cold.

"Be careful, Liam." Joe swam on, leading the way to the Zodiac.

VANESSA WAS HUDDLED at the side of the boat with Karine, watching McBrien have a beer with two men at the table.

They had touched her; groped her through her clothes. Laughed as she'd kept Karine behind her and away from their disgusting hands. When she had spit at them, McBrien had hit her again. This time the blow had knocked her to the deck.

"This one has some fire to her," one of the grotesque buyers had said.

"I'm sure we can find someone who will have a lot of fun finding a way to put that fire out," the other buyer had said.

All three men had laughed as if they'd just heard the funniest joke on the planet.

Vanessa had just stayed down on the deck. Karine had joined her, huddling against her side. The rain began to fall.

Out of the corner of her eye, she saw movement at the back of the boat. At first she thought it was Anderson and the big guy, Paul, bringing the girls out to be paraded in front of the buyers.

But then she realized it was people scurrying the other way, toward the back from the hull. Someone dressed all in black caught her eye.

Liam. Or maybe Joe or Derek. *They were here on the boat.*

"Dwayne, Paul, hurry up!" McBrien yelled. "What's taking so long?"

Vanessa knew what was taking so long: Liam was getting those girls off the boat.

"Karine," Vanessa whispered directly into the girl's ear. "It's very important that you don't make any sudden moves or look over there, but Liam and his team are on board. They're getting the girls out."

Karine stopped crying. She nodded.

"I'm going to try to give them more time, if I can. Keep these guys distracted."

"No, Vanessa. They hurt you," Karine implored.

Vanessa didn't reply, just held the girl close to her. The men at the table kept drinking their beer and laughing at their own stupid jokes as if they were at a barbecue rather than in the process of destroying lives.

"Anderson, what the hell is going on? Hurry up!" McBrien yelled again when he'd finished his beer. Then he turned to the buyers. "I'm sorry. I'll go check on them myself."

Had Liam gotten the girls off the boat? Were they safe? Had he had enough time? Vanessa didn't know.

She stood and walked toward the sheriff. "McBrien, I've got to go to the bathroom."

"Shut up, Vanessa. Sit back down."

She grabbed his arm. "Really, it's an emergency."

McBrien's eyes narrowed as he looked at Vanessa then toward the stern of the boat. He pushed off her hand and began rushing toward the back.

"What is going on?" he snarled.

Vanessa tried to grab him again, but couldn't. McBrien only made it a couple of steps before he fell to the deck in a flying tackle from Karine. He immediately punched the girl and she flew off him and against the side of the boat. Vanessa also tried to stop him, but he just shrugged her off.

"McBrien, what the hell is going on?" one of the buyers asked, sitting more stiffly in his chair.

"Yeah, why don't you tell the man what's going on?" The voice came from the other side of the boat.

Liam.

He was here and he had a gun pointed right at the sheriff.

Thank God.

McBrien stopped his walk toward the stern and turned around to face Liam.

"Ah, Agent Goetz. I have to admit, I'm a little surprised to see you here. I thought you'd be out somewhere in Harper's Cove."

Liam just grinned as if he had nothing better to do than talk to McBrien. "I heard the party was here. Couldn't resist."

He turned his head just slightly toward the buyers, who had stood and had a panicked look in their eyes.

"You two just keep your hands far away from your body. I have no beef with you, just with him." Liam jerked his chin toward McBrien. "I think we can avoid any unnecessary hard feelings between us if you'll just leave now."

Vanessa wanted to howl her anger at the thought of those men—those men who had groped and humiliated her, who had obviously bought children from McBrien before, given their level of comfort with him—getting away. But she forced it down. Liam had a plan, and for whatever reason, that plan involved letting these guys go.

Maybe Webb was around nearby to pick them up. Maybe Liam just knew that the safety of the girls outweighed arresting these bastards right now. Whatever his plan, Vanessa would trust him.

"Yeah, we don't have any beef with you, either, man," one of the guys said as they turned, arms far from their torsos, toward their boat.

Liam nodded. "Glad we understand each other. Get out. Now."

The men walked full speed to their boat. Within a moment they had tossed the metal gangway that connected their boat to McBrien's and were pulling away.

"That had to have hurt, Mr. Super Agent," McBrien mocked. "Letting them go like that."

Liam now had the gun trained directly at the sheriff.

"I have no doubt you—or one of your two partners—will roll on them in an attempt to reduce your sentence. We'll get them."

Vanessa got herself off the deck and helped Karine to her feet. She backed them to the side of the boat, far from the line of fire between Liam and McBrien. She didn't want to take a chance on Karine getting hurt.

And she was very, very worried that McBrien did not look the least bit concerned that Liam was pointing a gun at him. That he was about to be arrested on some pretty hefty charges.

"McBrien, put your hands on your head. You're

under arrest." Liam took a step closer. "Anything you say can and will be used against you in a court of law—"

"Let me stop you right there. I have something that might change your feelings on this whole situation," McBrien interrupted.

Liam rolled his eyes. "I'm pretty sure nothing is going to change my feelings about arresting your ass."

Something at the stern of the boat caught Vanessa's attention. It was Joe coming up the ladder they'd used to take the girls out. Good, now Liam had backup.

"If you think I'm going to let you reach for anything near your body, you can think again, McBrien," Liam continued. "I don't care what you have to show me. If you make a sudden move, you're dead."

"No, it's right here in my hand." McBrien's smile was chilling. He opened his hand to show a small mechanical device in his palm.

"Yeah, what's that?" Liam asked.

"It's a detonator for the explosives I rigged to this boat."

Chapter Twenty-Four

From the edge of his peripheral vision, Liam saw Vanessa blanch and pull Karine closer to her, but he kept his focus on McBrien. They had tried to account for as many scenarios as they could when they'd planned this rescue op.

McBrien being willing to blow himself and everyone else on the boat straight to hell hadn't been one of them.

"You probably don't want to shoot me, because it's a pressure detonator and I just armed it. If I let pressure off this lever, everything goes boom. Your precious Vanessa. That brat. All the girls below deck…"

"You," Liam finished for him.

"Me, too, that's true." McBrien shrugged. "It's a chance I'm willing to take."

Liam saw Joe walk silently behind McBrien. He knew Joe could hear everything McBrien was saying, and would know not to take the man out. It wasn't worth the risk if they had any other options.

Joe began moving toward Karine and Vanessa. If he could get them off the boat, it would be completely clear.

Thunder cracked immediately over them and rain began to fall in earnest. The noise might work to their advantage. Liam needed to keep McBrien's attention on him while Joe got Vanessa and Karine to safety.

"Really? What about your partners? You going to take them out as well as yourself? Seems a little overkill, if you'll pardon the pun," Liam said, relaxing his posture slightly and shifting a little more to the side so McBrien's focus was away from where Joe was joining the women.

"We both know what happens to me if I go to prison. Previous law-enforcement officers doing time in a maximum-security facility? I won't last long and my life would be a living hell while I do."

That sounded just fine to Liam, but he forced himself not to say so.

"It doesn't have to be that way," Liam said instead. "We can talk to a judge, make it so you aren't put in with the general population. There are other options. Don't do anything rash."

It was an empty promise and McBrien knew it.

"No!" He took a step forward, waving his arm. "There are only two options. You let me go or everyone on board dies."

The older man was turning to look at the other side of the boat.

"McBrien, what the hell do you want me to do?" Liam shouted through the rain to bring the man's attention back to him. "Am I just going to swim with a bunch of girls? I can't let you go. This is the only boat."

McBrien didn't know the girls were gone. Let him keep thinking he had the upper hand. Liam saw Joe begin to lower Karine into the water. Good. As soon as she and Vanessa were off, he and Joe had more options.

None of them were particularly good options, but they were options.

"I know you have a boat out there somewhere, Goetz. Even if you were idiotic enough to think you could swim all the way here, you had to have something to take the girls back in."

"The plan was to take the girls in this boat. To arrest you and whoever you were working with and bring the boat back to shore." The lie came easily from Liam's lips.

"You always were a pain in the ass, Goetz," McBrien said. "Even when you were a no-good teenager just looking for trouble. No one could believe it when you scored the princess of the island.

"I know your daddy had a fit when you first brought Goetz ho—" McBrien turned toward Vanessa as he said it, just in time to see Joe help her over the side and into the water.

"What the—"

Joe and Liam both immediately took action.

Joe threw Vanessa into the water.

Liam flew forward to tackle McBrien.

Joe was running toward them.

But it was too late.

As Liam tackled him, McBrien began to laugh hysterically.

"I'm glad to take you with me if I have to go," McBrien whispered. Madness lingered in his eyes as he lifted his hand to show Liam the lever that was now no longer compressed.

The boat was going to blow.

Liam bounced to his feet knowing he wouldn't make it off in time. But then Joe hit him in the hardest flying tackle he'd ever felt. They both flew over the side of the boat as fire and unbearable pressure suddenly surrounded them, accelerating them through the air.

Liam felt heat burn his body, sear his lungs, before they hit the water.

Then he felt and saw nothing but blackness.

VANESSA HADN'T BEEN prepared for Joe's help over the side of the boat to turn into a sudden, painful shove, but she'd known what it meant.

McBrien was going to blow up the boat.

She grabbed Karine and they began to swim as hard and fast as they could.

They were still close enough to feel the searing heat from the blast, to feel the momentum as it pushed them what seemed like a very far distance in the water.

Vanessa grabbed for Karine again, called for her, as debris flew all around them. For one terrified moment she couldn't find the girl in the darkness and rain, but then she broke through the surface a few yards from Vanessa, sputtering.

Vanessa swam to Karine and got beneath her, trying to support her weight so she could catch her breath.

"Are you okay?" Vanessa asked. "Are you hurt anywhere?"

"No, I'm okay," Karine murmured between breaths.

A piece of the boat, obviously buoyant from how it bobbed merrily in the water, drifted toward them. Still supporting Karine as best she could, Vanessa kicked out her leg to try to grab it. She succeeded in getting it to float directly in front of them and deposited Karine's weight on it. The girl grabbed and held on.

The rain was pouring. Vanessa could hardly figure out where the boat—now in small pieces all around them—had once been. How far had the momentum pushed them? Which way should they swim? Which direction was land or the Zodiac?

And, oh, God, had Liam gotten off the boat before it exploded? Vanessa had no idea.

The water was rough from the storm and the explosion. Vanessa tried yelling, but received no response. She tamped down the panic that threatened to overwhelm her. Her life, Karine's life, depended on her not panicking.

But looking around the dark, choppy waters with no one around and no land in sight? It was tough not to panic.

Vanessa wasn't sure what to do. Were they better off picking a direction and swimming toward it? Was it better to wait here in case someone brought rescue vehicles?

Karine was resting, exhausted, on the boat plank Vanessa had grabbed. She didn't blame the girl. Every bone in her own body ached. And the water was cold.

It was only October, so the cold at least wasn't life-threatening. But that didn't mean it wasn't uncomfortable. And the rain certainly wasn't helping.

Vanessa hoisted herself up on the floating boat piece as far as she could to look around. All she needed was one glimpse of a light or one sound from a location she could pinpoint and it would give her somewhere to go.

She couldn't see or hear anything. She sank back down in the water.

Karine was shivering against the plank. They would swim, or at least kick while holding the plank. That would help generate body heat. They would move in the direction of the explosion.

Or at least what Vanessa hoped was that direction.

"Let's kick, Karine," Vanessa said. "It will help us stay warm. We'll go toward where Liam and the other girls are."

"O-okay." Karine's voice was weak. "Are they dead?"

"No, sweetie." Vanessa touched her shoulder with hands that weren't very steady because of cold or fear or both. "They're alive. Everyone is alive. Liam and Joe and Derek got the girls off the boat long before the bad man blew it up. They're okay. They're all okay."

Vanessa prayed it was true.

They swam in silence, in the rain. Both of them held on to the plank and kicked. They swam for five minutes, ten minutes, longer. Vanessa lost track.

They had to have passed where the boat had been; it couldn't have been this far. Vanessa couldn't see anything. She couldn't hear anything. The storm was drowning everything out.

What time was it? Was it anywhere near dawn? It had been after midnight when McBrien had taken them from the house, so maybe it was about 3:00 a.m. now. Still a couple of hours before the sun would start to rise and she could hopefully see where land was.

She felt a sting against one of her legs, then another one. Jellyfish. The Roanoke Sound was famous for them in the late summer and early fall. They weren't dangerous or their sting even terribly painful, just uncomfortable.

Karine was falling asleep on the plank. Both had long since stopped kicking.

"Karine, let's see if we can get our weights totally on the plank. See if it will support us both, okay? Then we can rest."

Karine nodded weakly then shifted her weight more onto the float. Almost immediately upon finding herself in a horizontal position, she closed her eyes, drawing her legs up to her chest for warmth.

Vanessa pulled her weight onto the floating plank, too, but as soon as she did it began to sink. It wasn't buoyant enough to hold both of them. She slid back off to keep Karine from going under.

"Should I get off?" Karine murmured, barely lifting her head.

Vanessa felt another sting. There was no way she would subject Karine to this; she'd been through enough. Vanessa could survive a few jellyfish stings. It would soon be morning. All Vanessa had to do was to hang on. Literally and figuratively. This wasn't the *Titanic*. Vanessa wouldn't freeze.

She lost track of time as she was stung over and over. No one sting was unbearable but, taken altogether, her legs began to feel as if they were on fire. Tears rolled down her cheeks at first but eventually dried up, too.

She just wanted to sleep yet knew she couldn't. If she did, she would fall off the board and drown. She had to hang on.

But it became harder, more agonizing. She whimpered as she tried to move her legs. They felt stiff and awkward. And incredibly painful.

She laid her head to rest on the board, long past caring about the temperature of the water. She could see the subtle change of texture in the darkness furthest away.

The sun was beginning to rise.

Soon Vanessa would be able to get her bearings, to know which way to find the shore. Unfortunately she wasn't going to be able to do anything once she knew. There was no way she could swim or kick. She could barely move at all. The stings were unbearable now.

She kept her head where it lay, close to Karine in case the girl woke up. Vanessa just tried to hold on but didn't know how long she would be able to.

Chapter Twenty-Five

Liam had never known fear like this. All-encompassing, wrapping him from head to toe.

They couldn't find Vanessa and Karine.

Liam would be dead if it wasn't for Joe. His tackle momentum had gotten them both off the boat before the detonation. And although the protective material from their specialty wet suits had shielded them from the worst of the blast, Joe had still been injured. He was on his way to the hospital right now with burns and a puncture wound. But he was conscious and had assured Liam he would be fine.

Derek and the girls were all right—they were scared and wanted to see Karine—but none of them had been hurt in the blast. They, also, were on their way to the hospital, Derek in charge of their custody for the time being.

Now Liam was out on the water, along with Webb and the Coast Guard, looking for Vanessa and Karine. This storm was making everything more complicated, especially since they couldn't use helicopters for the search effort.

"Sir, this will be much more effective during the day. The sun should be up in just a couple hours."

But Liam couldn't stand the thought of them out here, maybe hurt, definitely scared, for even a minute longer than they had to be.

"The water temperature, even with prolonged exposure, should not be life-threatening. Barring injury, of course," the man continued.

Liam set his jaw. "It's still damn cold, I'm sure, especially with their lack of body mass. We keep looking."

"Yes, sir."

Liam kept searching for anything that might catch his attention in the night. Any changes in texture in the darkness or items that might reflect light. Once every thirty seconds or so, they blew a whistle, although it was probably pretty muffled by the storm.

"Do you know how far they were from the boat when the blast occurred?" another rescue team member asked.

"They were far enough. They're still alive."

"I'm sure that's true," the man muttered.

"They were farther than Joe or I were."

Everyone was wise enough not to mention that Joe was currently in the hospital, despite the protective layer his wet suit had provided. Vanessa and Karine hadn't had that protection.

They hadn't had Liam and Joe's strength or their survival training.

Liam refused to admit that at some point this might become a body recovery effort rather than a search and rescue mission.

Vanessa Epperson was alive. Nothing else was acceptable. And when he found her, he wasn't sure he was ever going to be able to let her out of his sight again.

They began to make wider sweeps as the night went on. If Vanessa had swum in the right direction, where the boat had exploded was less than a mile off shore… But on a stormy night, in rough seas, finding that direction might have been difficult. If she had swum in the wrong direction, she could be headed out of the cove and toward the open water of the Atlantic. That could prove deadly.

How long could they swim and which direction had they gone? Those were the questions everyone tried to answer to direct their attention in the search.

The sun had just pinkened the sky the slightest bit when something caught Liam's eye through his binoculars. He threw his focus to whatever it was he'd seen in the water.

"Southwest about five hundred yards," he called

out. "I'm not sure it's them, but there's definitely something in the water."

Liam didn't let his hopes get too high. They had found various pieces of wreckage in the water throughout the evening. But this was definitely a good-sized chunk.

The boat operator turned and sped in the direction Liam had indicated. A few moments later Liam's hands clenched on the binoculars.

It was them.

Karine was curled up on a plank of some sort—obviously a piece of the boat—mostly out of the water. Vanessa had evidently dragged the top half of her body over the plank when she'd become too exhausted to do anything else.

But even from several yards away, he could see that their faces were out of the water. That was at least promising.

Although their lack of movement was not.

The Coast Guard's boat was able to pull directly up beside them. Liam didn't even wait for permission or instruction; he just lowered himself into the water so he could be directly beside Vanessa.

"Vanessa?" He shook her softly but she didn't move. "Vanessa, wake up, honey."

Nightmares from the other night when Vanessa hadn't been breathing in the water flashed through Liam's mind. He tried to find a pulse.

"Mr. Liam?" Karine lifted her head weakly and looked at him.

"Hey, Karine. Are you okay?" He asked the question while moving Vanessa's thick hair out of the way so he could find her pulse.

"Miss Vanessa hasn't talked in a long time."

Liam swallowed his panic. There were a lot of reasons Vanessa might not have spoken. Exhaustion being one of them.

When he couldn't seem to find a pulse at her throat, he moved his hand to her wrist.

C'mon, baby.

It had been the same words he had used when he'd needed her to breathe before.

And it seemed to work again. He found her pulse beating in her wrist. Thank God.

"She's still breathing, Karine. Okay? We need to get her on the boat and back to the hospital. You, too."

Karine nodded. Two more men from the rescue team had joined them in the water.

"These guys are going to help you onto the boat. Is it okay if they touch you? I'll be right here, but I've got to help Vanessa, too."

Karine nodded again, although Liam could see her stiffen.

"Good girl."

They hoisted Vanessa onto the vessel and Liam climbed up the ladder. The men assisted Karine but tried to touch her as little as possible, aware of her situation.

They laid Vanessa on a small cot in the section

of the boat that wasn't exposed to the elements. One of the men wrapped a blanket around Karine as she sat on the floor.

Liam turned all his attention toward Vanessa as the boat sped toward shore. She still hadn't moved, hadn't made a sound. He, along with the ship's medic, peeled her out of her wet clothes, checking her for injuries while wrapping her in a blanket.

Liam saw the tiny wounds on Vanessa's legs at the same time the medic did. Dozens and dozens of tiny welts.

"Sea nettle stings," the medic said. "Sound is full of them this time of year."

Anybody growing up in the Outer Banks knew about this type of jellyfish. They were a nuisance but generally not life-threatening.

Of course, Liam had never seen this many stings before. And he couldn't imagine how painful sting after sting would be. "Is there anything we can do for her?"

"She's probably in a sort of toxic shock," the man replied. "We'll radio ahead to the ambulance and hospital to notify them of the situation. They'll have a specialist standing by."

The man turned to go make the radio contact.

"She's still breathing. Still here," he said, turning to look back from the steps leading up to the control room. "That's the most important thing."

Liam nodded, then sat on the cot and gathered

Vanessa up in his arms. Her body was cold to the touch.

A few moments later Karine scurried over from her spot on the floor to a place on the floor closer to the cot. "Will she be okay?" Karine's voice was hoarse.

Liam didn't know if it was from emotion or from what she'd been through. He reached down and touched the girl's head. "Vanessa is strong. She's a fighter."

He pulled Vanessa closer to him as if to will her to do just that. "Did you get stung by anything, Karine?"

"No. I was on top of floating board." Karine began to cry. "I should have let Vanessa up, too. I did not know fish were hurting her."

Liam stroked the girl's head again. "I know, honey. Vanessa is sometimes too stubborn for her own good. But she wanted you to be safe. I'm so glad you're safe."

"But Vanessa—"

"Shh. Vanessa will be fine, you just watch."

Liam prayed it would be true. The longer she lay so still in his arms, the more he worried.

"We got the other girls out, too," he told Karine. "You'll be able to see them as soon as we get to the hospital."

That at least helped clear up the tears. Liam moved his hand back to Vanessa to move strands of wet hair from her face and to wrap her more securely in the blanket.

"C'mon, baby, wake up," he whispered against her temple, bringing her closer to him. At least her skin wasn't as cold now.

Once they reached the dock, an ambulance was waiting to take them to the hospital. The EMT looked as if he was going to question Liam's right to be in the ambulance, but quickly put his questions to rest with one look at Liam's face. There was no way in hell Liam wasn't riding in the vehicle with Vanessa.

"She's coming with us, too." He pointed to Karine, who jumped in the ambulance with them. The EMT quickly closed the door before anyone else got in.

Vanessa didn't move the entire way, although her pulse and breathing remained steady.

Liam stayed with her as long as he could once they got to the hospital before a doctor told him he would have to wait in the waiting room. They would provide an update as soon as they could.

Liam let the nurse know where he could be found for the next few minutes in case anyone came out with an update about Vanessa, then took Karine to see the rest of the girls. They were all being kept together, guarded by Derek and a whole slew of kind-faced nurses and social workers.

The girls were ecstatic to see Karine. They all hugged and sobbed and held on to each other.

These girls were bonded together in ways that no one else would ever be able to completely understand.

As Liam watched from the doorway, touched but anxious to get back to the waiting area in case Vanessa needed him, Derek joined him.

"Vanessa?"

"Unconscious. Multiple sea nettle stings, prolonged exposure to the elements...who knows what else? But she's breathing. I'll take that for now. I need to get back for when the doctor comes out with a report."

"I'll stay here with the girls. I just want to double-check that everything is in order with them before I release them from my custody."

"Thanks, Derek. Does everything seem all right with them medically, all things considered?"

"All are suffering from dehydration." Derek grimaced. "And they've all been assaulted, except for the youngest one."

Liam looked over at the little girl who had clung to him while they swam. She was looking at him. Thank God she had been spared that trauma, at least. The rest was bad enough.

"But it looks like all of them are going to be okay. We've already made contact with the Estonian embassy to figure out how we can make sure the girls are returned to their parents. If the parents aren't the ones who sold them to the traffickers in the first place."

It was difficult to think of parents doing that to their own children, but Liam knew it happened more than people expected, especially in situations where the rest of the family was starving.

Liam nodded. "Let's stay on top of that. I want to make sure none of those girls is sent back if it's just going to result in the same thing happening."

"Oh, believe me," Derek said. "Molly would have my head if I sent even one of those girls home to a bad family situation. I just hope I'm not about to become the adoptive father to seven teenage girls."

Liam chuckled. "Nothing less than you deserve. Speaking of...how's Joe?"

"Fine. Already flirting with the nurses. I think they'll release him tomorrow. Burns on his back and a puncture wound from some debris, but nothing serious."

"Thank God for the Kevlar wet suits."

"Absolutely. Would've been much worse otherwise." Derek slapped him on the back. "Get back to Vanessa. I can tell that's where you want to be. I've got everything covered here. I'll keep you posted if something changes. You do the same about her."

Liam nodded and jogged out of the room and down the hall to the emergency waiting area. He checked with the nurse, just in case, but found he hadn't missed any updates from the doctor. He settled in to wait, hoping it wouldn't be too long.

The longer he waited, the more worried he became. That many jellyfish stings...could they be toxic? Was she having an allergic reaction? Did she have a head trauma they didn't know about?

There were so many possibilities. Many of them terrifying.

Vanessa's parents were rushing through the Emergency entrance just as the doctor came through the waiting room door to provide an update.

"What's going on, Doctor?" George Epperson demanded. "What's happening with our daughter?"

"I'm Dr. Turner. Who are you?" the doctor asked Liam.

"Her fiancé." Liam told the lie without batting an eye. There was no way he was going to be kept out of information loop when it came to Vanessa.

Both her parents turned to stare at him but neither said anything.

"Is your name Liam?"

"Yes."

"Good, I'm glad you're here," the doctor said. "Miss Epperson has been asking for you in her sleep. I think she will find your presence comforting."

"I'm going back there right now."

The doctor touched his arm. "They're moving her to a private room and need a little while. You can go back there in just a minute. Let me give you an update first."

Vanessa was calling for him. That was really the only update Liam needed. But he forced himself to listen. Maybe there was a complication he needed to know about.

He turned back to the doctor. "Okay."

"Well, first..." the doctor said, "let me assure you that Vanessa is going to be fine. And at this point it does not look like her pregnancy was jeopardized by last night's events."

Chapter Twenty-Six

Liam grabbed the counter next to him, trying not to be obvious in his need for support. Vanessa's parents had no such reservations. Her mother, Rhonda, swayed into George, grabbing his arm.

"Pregnancy?" Rhonda asked.

"Did you know about this?" George asked Liam.

"No. Not this time, either." His eyes narrowed at the older man.

George had the good grace to at least look away.

Liam turned toward Dr. Turner. "Are you sure, Doctor? I don't know much about pregnancy tests and hospitals, but if Vanessa's pregnant, it would not be by much—only a few days."

"Interesting." Dr. Turner looked at the chart again. "Vanessa definitely has traces of hCG—the pregnancy hormone—in her bloodstream, enough for a viable pregnancy. We had to test for it when deciding the best course for treating the stings.

There's no chance she could've been pregnant, say, roughly ten days?"

Liam remembered what Vanessa had told him about not having any other lovers for so long. "Not a chance. Does that mean your test could be wrong and she's not pregnant?"

The doctor looked at his chart again. "No, the opposite, in fact."

What the hell did that even mean? The opposite of *not pregnant* was pregnant, right? But it was too early to tell that.

"Let me make sure these hCG numbers are right and I'll get back to you."

"What about her other injuries?" Liam asked. "Is she going to be okay?"

"Yes. Although painful, the stings of the *chrysaora quinquecirrha*, or what we know around here as a sea nettle, aren't fatal unless you have an allergic reaction. She shouldn't have any permanent damage from the stings."

Liam released a breath he didn't even know he had been holding.

"It was actually just bad luck on Ms. Epperson's part that she was even exposed to them. Given another two weeks, it would be too cold for them to be in the water." Dr. Turner shrugged. "Of course, given another two weeks, the water might have been cold enough to do Vanessa much greater harm."

"So why is she still unconscious?" Liam asked.

"Mind protecting itself. We estimate she was stung over four dozen times—the pain was immense, I'm sure. Coupled with the elements she'd been exposed to, not to mention she'd been kidnapped, right?"

Liam could see George and Rhonda's shocked looks from the corners of his eyes.

"Let's just say she'd had a pretty traumatic night. Her body needed a break and her mind gave it to her. Now that she's warm, hydrated and not in pain, she's starting to wake up."

And Liam needed to get in there.

"I'll be back with the hCG numbers after we run the test again. I don't want to confuse the situation for anyone."

She was either pregnant or she wasn't pregnant. It wasn't too confusing, as far as Liam was concerned. He just wanted to know which. Actually, right now he didn't even care about that. He just wanted to see Vanessa.

As he turned to walk down the hall, Rhonda Epperson grabbed his arm.

"I know Vanessa doesn't want to see us," she said. "And we're not going to force ourselves in there and upset her even more. It sounds like she's been through enough."

Liam nodded. "I'll tell her you're here. Tell her you're worried. She's not heartless. Just stubborn."

"I suppose she told you about what happened eight years ago. The miscarriage...how I mislead you," George said. "For what it's worth, I am sorry. I honestly thought both of you would just get over it."

Tears welled in Rhonda's eyes. "But Vanessa never did."

"If it helps, I never did, either," Liam said.

"I was wrong to interfere like that," George said. "I was just trying to protect my only daughter from someone I thought might be of questionable repute."

Liam could understand that. He didn't agree with Epperson's measures, but he could definitely understand his motivation. "I'll talk to Vanessa once she's awake. Explain. Maybe it's time for all of us to put the past behind us and just concentrate on the future."

"Do you really think it's possible she's pregnant?" Rhonda asked.

"It could be possible, just not likely that she's far enough along for them to detect it. So I think it's probably an error."

Both George and Rhonda looked crestfallen. Evidently it didn't bother them anymore that Vanessa could be permanently linked to Liam through having a child.

That didn't matter because, child or not, he planned to be permanently linked to Vanessa for the rest of his life. All he had to do was convince Vanessa. Which he planned to do starting right now.

EVERYTHING FELT FUZZY as Vanessa awoke. Thoughts seemed to process slowly, almost one at a time.

She wasn't in the water anymore. She didn't have to swim. Those jellyfish weren't stinging her anymore. Karine was safe. All the girls were safe. Liam was right here next to her.

How did she know all this? She opened her eyes just the slightest bit.

She knew it because Liam was lying next to her on her hospital bed whispering these facts over and over in her ear.

She turned toward him. "Hey," she whispered.

She felt his lips move against the side of her face. "There you are."

"How long have I been out?"

"We're not sure how long you were in the water. But you've been in the hospital a couple of hours."

"Have you been with me the whole time?"

Liam pulled her closer. "As soon as they would let me in. You were stung a lot of times and there were some…considerations when treating you."

"What sort of considerations?"

Liam shifted. "I didn't really understand it. I'll let the doctor explain."

That didn't sound promising, but Vanessa let it go.

"And the girls really are all safe?"

"Yes, we got them out safely. I had a tracker app on Karine's phone, so once we knew how to use it, we were able to get to you."

Vanessa explained how McBrien had found them at the house, using Andrea's name.

"McBrien was smart. If we hadn't already gotten the girls out, he probably would've been able to get away. He definitely had no plan to go to prison, that's for sure."

The doctor came into the room. Liam didn't even shift except to pull Vanessa closer.

"I'm Dr. Turner, Vanessa. I see your fiancé found you."

Fiancé? Vanessa looked at Liam. He just shrugged.

"Thanks, Doc," Liam said. "I had no problems finding her at all."

"How are you feeling?"

"Nothing hurts, so that's good, right?"

"We have you on some pain medication through your IV, nothing too strong, given the situation, but it's good you're not in any discomfort. Given the nature of sea nettle stings, all pain should be completely gone by tomorrow anyway."

"Great, but given what *situation*?" She looked from Dr. Turner to Liam. What weren't they telling her?

"We double-checked those numbers I was telling you about before," the doctor said to Liam.

Vanessa sat all the way up. "What numbers? What's going on?"

Dr. Turner took a step closer. "Treating the sea

nettle stings was complicated by the fact that we found traces of hCG in your bloodstream."

She looked at Liam again then back at Dr. Turner. "What is hCG? Is that bad?"

"No." Dr. Turner shook his head. "It's the pregnancy hormone. Every pregnant woman has it in her blood."

"The pregnancy hormone…" Vanessa's voice trailed off, not sure she was actually understanding.

"Your fiancé thought it might be an incorrect test reading, since you couldn't be more than a few days pregnant."

"Yes, that's true. Is it even possible to tell this early?"

Dr. Turner nodded. "Yes, especially with a blood sample like we used. But what was even more interesting was the relatively high levels of hCG in your blood. That's what made us think you were further along in the pregnancy than you are."

"Is that bad?" Liam asked. "Dangerous?"

"No." Dr. Turner smiled. "High levels of hCG is usually indicative of a mis-estimated conception date or, as in your case, it means you're pregnant with multiples."

Vanessa couldn't seem to process what the doctor was saying. She looked at Liam again but he looked just as dumbfounded.

"What?" she finally asked.

The doctor patted her on the shoulder. "We

won't know for sure for a while yet, so everyone should be sure to take that into consideration, but it's highly likely that you're pregnant with twins."

Vanessa turned and stared at Liam, who was staring back at her. As if from a distance she heard the doctor excuse himself and walk out, closing the door behind him.

"You're pregnant," Liam whispered.

"I can't believe it."

"With *twins*."

Vanessa shook her head and put a hand over her stomach. "What does this mean?" It was almost too much to process, given everything that had happened in the past twenty-four hours.

"It means we need to finish that conversation we started the other day at your apartment."

Vanessa tried to pull away. She didn't want to talk about Liam with other women. "Liam, look—"

"No, I want you to hear what I have to say, Nessa. I should've said it years ago, and I would've said it now anyway, even if the doctor hadn't just come in here and told us we're going to be tied to each other's lives forever with the baby— babies—you have inside you."

He cupped her face. "I'm not going to let our pride, or miscommunication, or well-meaning family keep us apart any longer. We lost eight years of our life together, and I don't want to lose a minute more."

He brought his lips to hers and kissed her. Softly. Full of tenderness. The passion, for once, took a backseat. "Yes, there were other women. Too many. But none of them was you, Nessa. I thought I was being a playboy, enjoying my freedom. But really I was just killing time until I finally grew enough brains to come back and get you."

"Liam—"

He kissed her again. "And I was coming for you, Nessa. I just didn't know it yet. Your call gave me the excuse I needed. I love you. I've never stopped loving you. I should've fought for you then."

"I should've fought for you, too," she whispered. He wasn't solely to blame in this.

"I will spend the rest of my life fighting for our family. If there is one thing the past twenty-four hours has showed me, it's that I have no desire to live without you."

"But what about our jobs? You live in—"

"I. Don't. Care." He punctuated each word with another kiss. "I will quit my job and work at a convenience store before I will be separated from you again. Baby, babies, or just you and me—I don't care. I'm not leaving your side again, unless I hear the words directly from you for me to go. And even then I don't think I can do it."

These were the words Vanessa had dreamed of hearing for eight years. "Well, I don't think you have to worry about that because I don't plan to say them."

"Good."

There was a soft tap on the door. Derek peeked his head in. "Sorry to interrupt. We heard you were awake and someone was very interested in seeing you."

Karine flew in from behind Derek. "Vanessa!"

Vanessa opened her arms and the girl ran into them. Liam got up from the bed to allow the girls to embrace.

"I was so worried. I am so sorry I did not help more with swimming."

Vanessa smoothed Karine's hair. "No, no. Don't say that. We made it. Everybody made it. That's what counts."

Vanessa looked over at the doorway, where a little girl was standing next to Derek. "Who's that?" She smiled at the little girl.

"That's Tallinn. She's one of the girls from the boat. The youngest one I told you about."

"Tallinn demanded to see Liam," Derek said. "Especially when she found out Karine was coming here."

Liam made his way around the bed and knelt in front of Tallinn so they were close to the same height. "Hey, sweetie, how are you doing?"

The little girl looked down at the floor. Vanessa's heart melted as Liam put a finger under Tallinn's chin and smiled at her.

"I'm glad you're here," he said. "Want to come sit over here with me?"

Vanessa didn't know if the girl understood what Liam was saying, but she definitely understood the kindness in his voice. Liam sat on Vanessa's hospital bed and reached down to hoist Tallinn so she was sitting up there with them. A few moments later Liam was showing the girl how to make the bed move up and down. Soon the girl was giggling softly and playing with the buttons.

Liam would make a great father. Vanessa had no doubt about it.

He caught her looking at him.

"We've got to get these girls back to their families. Make sure they're safe. Then we're getting married," he said softly to her.

"Better late than never," she whispered back. "And in case you were wondering, I love you, too. Always have."

He winked. "I know."

One Year Later

VANESSA AND LIAM stood in the judge's chambers, the beautiful Rocky Mountains of Colorado Springs visible outside the window.

Vanessa hadn't made Liam go through on his promise to work at a convenience store so they could be together, although she honestly believed he would have if she had demanded to stay in the

Outer Banks. But she knew his work at Omega Sector Critical Response Division was too important to him—too important in general—for him to quit. They'd bought a house here six months ago, since one look at Liam's bachelor pad had her decreeing she would never live there, nor allow any of her children to.

Liam had readily agreed.

It had taken two months of cutting through bureaucracy and red tape before they had been able to get the girls back to their families in Estonia. Vanessa had sworn she would never touch her parents' money, but she'd been wrong. When proper channels weren't working quickly enough to get the girls home, Vanessa found that her parents' money helped things work much faster. She'd had no qualms about using it for the girls.

Liam had helped her work through a lot of the anger with her parents. They had wanted to protect her, he'd explained to her more than once. Anything they'd done, as wrong as it might have been, had been done out of love. Vanessa would always mourn the years—and life—lost, but she could at least see his point and had begun to let them back into her life.

When she'd found out that her parents had set up funds to pay for all the girls' medical bills, had made sure they had one of the best therapists in Estonia to help them, and had set up college funds for all of them, she had given up the last hardness she'd held against them. These were her children's grandparents.

Her parents were here with them now in the judge's chamber, each holding one of their grandsons. Twins. Born four months ago. Healthy and perfect.

"Weren't you just in here a few months ago?" the judge asked.

"Yes, Your Honor," Liam replied. "Since you had made our marriage official, we were hoping you'd make our family official, too."

The older man raised one eyebrow at them. "I'm glad to see you don't have half of Colorado Springs here with you today like last time."

They had wanted to get married before the babies came, but between getting the girls back home, moving across the country and everything else that had been going on, neither of them had had the time or inclination to plan a wedding.

They had decided to just get married in the judge's chambers: simple and to the point.

Vanessa had invited her parents, who had come. Liam had invited a couple of the guys from Omega Sector.

The next thing they knew, so many people had come to witness their nuptials that the judge's chamber had been completely filled. The judge had ordered them all downstairs to the courtroom, and had performed the ceremony there.

Vanessa and Liam had both been touched by

how many people had wanted to show their support. And especially touched by the fact that George and Rhonda had flown Karine and her parents over for the ceremony.

Karine had stood as Vanessa's maid of honor. Derek as Liam's best man.

"No, sir," Vanessa answered the judge. "Just family today."

They had found the families of all the girls— had personally witnessed that they were good family situations with parents that had been distraught by their daughters' abductions—and had returned them all to loving homes.

All except little Tallinn.

She'd been an orphan, had been one before she'd been kidnapped, and had no family to return to.

When Vanessa found out, she hadn't known what to do. The thought of putting her back in an orphanage where the same thing could happen to her again... Vanessa hadn't been able to even stomach it.

"She'll stay with us. We'll adopt her," Liam had said.

It had taken money and time. And a special visa that had allowed Tallinn into the US because of the trafficking situation.

She now stood between Vanessa and Liam, holding each of their hands, having picked up English in the way only a child could, and smiled at the judge.

"I am happy to sign this final adoption decree

for you to join this family, Miss Tallinn." The judge smiled at the little girl. "Are you sure that's what you want? For them to become your mommy and daddy?"

Tallinn's grin was from ear to ear. "Yes, sir. Then I want ice cream. Baby brothers can't have any because they too little."

The judge chuckled. "Well, let me sign this so we can get on to other important things."

He signed the paper and handed it to Liam, who thanked him.

Tallinn ran off to see her mimi and granddad and baby brothers.

Liam wrapped an arm around Vanessa's waist and pulled her closer as they walked out of the chambers. "It wasn't the way we'd planned it, but we have a beautiful family, Mrs. Goetz."

Vanessa kissed him.

"Forever."

* * * * *

Janie Crouch's
OMEGA SECTOR: CRITICAL RESPONSE
miniseries continues next month with
MAN OF ACTION.
Look for it wherever Harlequin Intrigue books
and ebooks are sold!

LARGER-PRINT BOOKS!

HARLEQUIN

Presents®

GET 2 FREE LARGER-PRINT NOVELS PLUS 2 FREE GIFTS!

PASSION
GUARANTEED
SEDUCTION

LARGER-PRINT BOOKS!
GET 2 FREE LARGER-PRINT NOVELS PLUS
2 FREE GIFTS!

♥HARLEQUIN®

Romance

From the Heart, For the Heart

YES! Please send me 2 FREE LARGER-PRINT Harlequin® Romance novels and my 2 FREE gifts (gifts are worth about $10). After receiving them, if I don't wish to receive any more books, I can return the shipping statement marked "cancel." If I don't cancel, I will receive 4 brand-new novels every month and be billed just $5.09 per book in the U.S. or $5.49 per book in Canada. That's a savings of at least 15% off the cover price! It's quite a bargain! Shipping and handling is just 50¢ per book in the U.S. and 75¢ per book in Canada.* I understand that accepting the 2 free books and gifts places me under no obligation to buy anything. I can always return a shipment and cancel at any time. Even if I never buy another book, the two free books and gifts are mine to keep forever.

119/319 HDN GHWC

Name	(PLEASE PRINT)	

Address		Apt. #

City	State/Prov.	Zip/Postal Code

Signature (if under 18, a parent or guardian must sign)

Mail to the **Reader Service:**
IN U.S.A.: P.O. Box 1867, Buffalo, NY 14240-1867
IN CANADA: P.O. Box 609, Fort Erie, Ontario L2A 5X3
Want to try two free books from another line?
Call 1-800-873-8635 or visit www.ReaderService.com.

* Terms and prices subject to change without notice. Prices do not include applicable taxes. Sales tax applicable in N.Y. Canadian residents will be charged applicable taxes. Offer not valid in Quebec. This offer is limited to one order per household. Not valid for current subscribers to Harlequin Romance Larger-Print books. All orders subject to credit approval. Credit or debit balances in a customer's account(s) may be offset by any other outstanding balance owed by or to the customer. Please allow 4 to 6 weeks for delivery. Offer available while quantities last.

Your Privacy—The Reader Service is committed to protecting your privacy. Our Privacy Policy is available online at www.ReaderService.com or upon request from the Reader Service.

We make a portion of our mailing list available to reputable third parties that offer products we believe may interest you. If you prefer that we not exchange your name with third parties, or if you wish to clarify or modify your communication preferences, please visit us at www.ReaderService.com/consumerchoice or write to us at Reader Service Preference Service, P.O. Box 9062, Buffalo, NY 14240-9062. Include your complete name and address.

LARGER-PRINT BOOKS!
GET 2 FREE LARGER-PRINT NOVELS PLUS
2 FREE GIFTS!

◆ HARLEQUIN®

super romance®

More Story...More Romance

YES! Please send me 2 FREE LARGER-PRINT Harlequin® Superromance® novels and my 2 FREE gifts (gifts are worth about $10). After receiving them, if I don't wish to receive any more books, I can return the shipping statement marked "cancel." If I don't cancel, I will receive 4 brand-new novels every month and be billed just $5.94 per book in the U.S. or $6.24 per book in Canada. That's a savings of at least 12% off the cover price! It's quite a bargain! Shipping and handling is just 50¢ per book in the U.S. or 75¢ per book in Canada.* I understand that accepting the 2 free books and gifts places me under no obligation to buy anything. I can always return a shipment and cancel at any time. Even if I never buy another book, the two free books and gifts are mine to keep forever.

132/332 HDN GHVC

Name _____
(PLEASE PRINT)

Address _____ Apt. # _____

City _____ State/Prov. _____ Zip/Postal Code _____

Signature (if under 18, a parent or guardian must sign) _____

Mail to the **Reader Service:**
IN U.S.A.: P.O. Box 1867, Buffalo, NY 14240-1867
IN CANADA: P.O. Box 609, Fort Erie, Ontario L2A 5X3

Want to try two free books from another line?
Call 1-800-873-8635 today or visit www.ReaderService.com.

* Terms and prices subject to change without notice. Prices do not include applicable taxes. Sales tax applicable in N.Y. Canadian residents will be charged applicable taxes. Offer not valid in Quebec. This offer is limited to one order per household. Not valid for current subscribers to Harlequin Superromance Larger-Print books. All orders subject to credit approval. Credit or debit balances in a customer's account(s) may be offset by any other outstanding balance owed by or to the customer. Please allow 4 to 6 weeks for delivery. Offer available while quantities last.

Your Privacy—The Reader Service is committed to protecting your privacy. Our Privacy Policy is available online at www.ReaderService.com or upon request from the Reader Service.

We make a portion of our mailing list available to reputable third parties that offer products we believe may interest you. If you prefer that we not exchange your name with third parties, or if you wish to clarify or modify your communication preferences, please visit us at www.ReaderService.com/consumerschoice or write to us at Reader Service Preference Service, P.O. Box 9062, Buffalo, NY 14240-9062. Include your complete name and address.

HSRLP15

WESTERN (WP) PROMISES

YES! Please send me **The Western Promises Collection** in Larger Print. This collection begins with 3 FREE books and 2 FREE gifts (gifts valued at approx. $14.00 retail) in the first shipment, along with the other first 4 books from the collection! If I do not cancel, I will receive 8 monthly shipments until I have the entire 51-book Western Promises collection. I will receive 2 or 3 FREE books in each shipment and I will pay just $4.99 US/ $5.89 CDN for each of the other four books in each shipment, plus $2.99 for shipping and handling per shipment. *If I decide to keep the entire collection, I'll have paid for only 32 books, because 19 books are FREE! I understand that accepting the 3 free books and gifts places me under no obligation to buy anything. I can always return a shipment and cancel at any time. My free books and gifts are mine to keep no matter what I decide.

272 HCN 3070 472 HCN 3070

Name	(PLEASE PRINT)	
Address		Apt. #
City	State/Prov.	Zip/Postal Code

Signature (if under 18, a parent or guardian must sign)

Mail to the **Reader Service:**

IN U.S.A.: P.O. Box 1867, Buffalo, NY 14240-1867
IN CANADA: P.O. Box 609, Fort Erie, Ontario L2A 5X3

* Terms and prices subject to change without notice. Prices do not include applicable taxes. Sales tax applicable in N.Y. Canadian residents will be charged applicable taxes. This offer is limited to one order per household. All orders subject to approval. Credit or debit balances in a customer's account(s) may be offset by any other outstanding balance owed by or to the customer. Please allow 4 to 6 weeks for delivery. Offer available while quantities last. Offer not available to Quebec residents.

Your Privacy—The Reader Service is committed to protecting your privacy. Our Privacy Policy is available online at www.ReaderService.com or upon request from the Reader Service.

We make a portion of our mailing list available to reputable third parties that offer products we believe may interest you. If you prefer that we not exchange your name with third parties, or if you wish to clarify or modify your communication preferences, please visit us at www.ReaderService.com/consumerschoice or write to us at Reader Service Preference Service, P.O. Box 9062, Buffalo, NY 14240-9062. Include your complete name and address.

WPBPA16R